The Desert Siren

The Desert Seas Book 1

Jessie Sadler

Tea With Coffee
—— Media ——

Tea With Coffee Media

The Desert Siren Copyright © 2022 by Jessie Sadler

Cover and Internal Design © 2022 by Tea With Coffee Media

Cover Design by Victoria Moxely/Tea With Coffee Media

Cover Images by Dreamstime

Internal Images © Kelsey Anne Lovelady via Canva and Paint Tool Sai

Tea With Coffee Media and the colophon are trademarks of Tea With Coffee Media

Published by Tea With Coffee Media

teawithcoffee.media

Cataloging-in-Publication Data is on file with the Library of Congress.

Published by Tea With Coffee Media

To Nikki, who challenged me to write this story. One word at a time.

To Cas, my biggest cheerleader and first ever fan- you helped me shape this world.

And to Nicole, who told me that this was "definitely good enough" and pushed me into this world,

Thank you.

Without you, I would never be giving this huge thank you to the amazing team that is TeaWithCoffee Media, for making this fantasy world sharable with the world.

Jessie Sadler

Contents

B orn of land and born of sea
        Sing the scales in harmony
    When tide is low and moon is strong
    She sings aloud a siren song
    Sung amidst the symphony
    The vocal choir is the key.
    A resonance of sea and land
    Force the fiends to show their hand
    Dissonance, discord it brings
    Tones in key she must still sing
    A show of brand-new melody
    United ends the tyranny.

*I*t started with a choice. To live or to die?

When I fell into the sea and drowned, the Mistress gave me this choice. To

continue to live, I would have to exchange my voice and soul in service to the sea for one hundred years. I was then transformed into a siren, reborn into her service. In one hundred years, my soul would be returned, and I could begin a second life.

I was brought to an underwater city to live amongst the sea creatures and merfolk. We were to be ready to complete her bidding when she called. I still had fifty-eight years left when I met him. He was a deaf sailor. The sirens and I sang to enchant his ship and crew, and all but him succumbed to the call and were sacrificed to the sea. He could not hear the sirens' song, and he was spared. He steered his lifeboat to a deserted island and battled the elements to survive.

He lived on that island, watching me as I watched him. One day he signed to me, and I realised we could communicate. I laid on the beach of that island, my tail drying in the sun and sand. I brought him fish to eat, and we learned to speak with each other. I became enamoured with him, and with time, I fell in love. I kept returning to that beach and spent the days with him, dipping into the water to keep my tail moist. I had a reason to keep living. A true love's kiss gave me legs, and I was a woman again, but my voice was still that of a siren. We stayed together surviving on that island. The other sirens were amazed at what had happened.

A passing ship rescued us both, a deaf and a mute stranded on a deserted island. They wondered how we had survived so long. We moved to his home inland, close to the sea.

A year passed and I gave birth to a beautiful baby girl with dark red hair and bright green eyes. We taught her to sign to communicate, but I heard her voice. I could not speak to my daughter. I worried whether she had any siren traits. I hummed a siren's lullaby, and she copied it. Her voice is beautiful. The first time I took her in the water, her skin turned to red scales and webbing and fins grew. She was part siren and had inherited my service to the sea. I convinced my husband to move to the desert.

The sirens came for me. First, they asked how I had escaped my service to the sea, or whether I would still have to return to fulfil my remaining years. They told me the Queen wanted me to come and tell them how to free themselves. I returned to Aquacity with the sirens. They tried to follow my lead, but when I wasn't able to sing anything different to change them, they locked me in my room.

I escaped, and returned to the surface, but when I went ashore, I could no longer change back to human. I told my husband to take her and leave the shore, move to the desert and to keep her out of any water! The witch herself came for me and dragged me back into the ocean. I remember my husband yelling and my daughter crying. Her cries caused the sea animals to come to her.

I hope they are okay, twenty-three years after I was taken from them. My daughter should be twenty-five years old, the same age as I was when I died.

I bolted upright, heart racing in my chest, as the nightmare lingered in my mind. My mouth was dry, my throat ached, and my palms and neck were damp. In my dark room, I reached for the glass of water on my nightstand and took a big gulp. *Water.* I thought, as I swallowed the cool relief. I was dreaming of water again. I remember it being dark, something grasped my ankle, and I was being dragged down into the dark watery abyss, screaming. *That explains the dry throat,* I thought, *Good thing dad is deaf.* He would never know I still had nightmares about drowning. Untangling the bed sheet that had twisted around my ankle as I left the offending place of rest, I pried open the window and leaned out into the night air. The warm desert wind did nothing to settle my racing heart.

My dad and I lived together in the dry Sonoran Desert. And for as long as I can remember, I've been terrified of water. That meant no swimming, no sprinklers, no baths, and always a very fast shower. I hated the thought of water, except to drink it- and even then, flavoured, please. Water and I were not a good match. I much prefer the cool sand that hides underneath the top layer, and often find myself digging my bare feet into the desert sand for comfort.

The sand outside called to me, so I headed out the front door in my pajamas. I let my feet dangle in the sand as I sat on the old tree swing, enjoying the night air.

My nightmares were brought forth due to my upcoming trip. I gripped the worn rope tightly as I swirled my feet in the sand. I was anxious, but dad said I needed to go and grow from it. I could advance my career; I could meet more professionals. But he still shocked me when he said to go.

An invitation from my music professor to a performance and contest on the musical arts. It was an adventure that should have excited me. I was working part time as a teaching assistant and vocal coach, and I led the student group choir as part of my undergraduate studies. My professor wanted me to go and make connections, to challenge my voice with others who were studying and already masters of their vocal cords. The problem was that this was all out of state and, most importantly, on an island.

Great! A university sponsored island vacation sounds like a wonderful trip, except for the fact that it was *an island*. In the middle of the ocean ... surrounded by water. It was my worst fear. If only I could swim in the sand. The cool, shifting sand. My feet circled beneath the grains, comforting me as they glided with the sway of the swing.

My father and I share the same fear of water, and it stems from traumatic memories. All I had was a hint of my mother's brown hair as she was sucked into the crashing waves. I remember screaming, and flailing fins. They must have been fish. My father moved us to the desert, and we never went into the water again. I began to hum my mom's song, the tune I remember from my childhood. I relaxed on the swing, feet in the sand, and the desert breeze blowing my auburn hair across my face. I tilted my head back and stared at the stars dotting the night sky.

I was both excited and nervous. I wanted to go and meet the other students who were crazy about music, singing and composing. But I was terrified. Could my love of singing overcome my fear of falling into the ocean, never to be seen again?

I remembered my dad's face when I showed him the invitation, the panic that crossed his face when he read it, but then he rearranged it into a smile.

"A symposium? Is that like a symphony? But with posiums instead of phonies?" he signed.

"Very funny." I signed back, even as I laughed, rolling my eyes. For a deaf man, he sure liked to tell dad jokes.

"It's an education event with people in your field presenting their research, their advancements, and their techniques. It's pretty much an opportunity to show off a little, but you also get to meet and greet your peers and teachers in your field."

"Very nice, so do you have a speaking role or do you just sit and listen to what others say?"

"We were invited as a choir to perform."

"Hmm. This says an all-expenses paid trip," he looks up at me. "Are you going to go?"

"You're not upset?!" I cried out, confused, then remembered to sign it to him.

"Why would I be upset? My smart daughter, who studied hard and practiced music every day. Who sang her heart out and teaches others to do the same. You deserve to be recognized for your accomplishments. You love music. And I don't blame you. If I could hear,

I'm sure I'd love your voice too. If you want to go, you SHOULD go." He sat back and I observed him.

He was trying to encourage me, but he gripped the chair arm so hard his knuckles were white, his smile forced. He was lying to cover his fear.

"I want to go. But it's on an island. I have no idea how I would do there." I replied. It's also during storm season, and I have a hundred and one things to complete here and..." I trailed off, looking for another excuse.

"There's only one excuse, Sahara, and you'll kick yourself in the ass if you don't try and go. Fear isn't a good enough excuse. "

"But Dad!"

"But nothing. You're twenty-four years old."

"Twenty-five."

"Okay, twenty-five years old. You've never left the desert. You've had one relationship, and pretty much absorb yourself in your studies. This is a part of your studies. You should want to go and travel, meet people, and experience life. I want to see you grow and expand your horizons. But." He paused, "I still want you to be very careful."

My eyes welled up in tears. He was my dad, and he wanted to see me grow and succeed. He wrapped me in a tight embrace, and I understood. I needed to take this journey.

It would change me in so many ways.

"I'll always remember, Dad, you can drown in a bowl of soup."

I meticulously packed my belongings, double and triple checking to be sure I had everything I could need. The furthest I'd travelled was to Nevada for a Vegas choir competition. We had done well but lost in the semi-finals and never made it to Washington. The Phoenix airport was as busy as ever, the hot sun bearing down on me. I nervously got through airport security, their scrutinizing looks and pokes and prods making me feel quite uncomfortable.

I lined up at the gate with the others from school traveling with me. My professor showed up about twenty minutes before boarding time. -

"I had to pay extra to ship the instruments carefully" she told me. "You're so lucky your instrument is free of charge and a carry-on!" she joked.

"Yeah, how fortunate." I nervously laughed with her.

The gate agent called for boarding, and we all lined up, were scanned, and entered the little metal tube with wings. Okay, it was large. Roomier than I expected, but still cozy with your neighbour. I threw my backpack up into the overhead bin and sat down, drawing my headphones out of my pocket, and putting them in my ears. I opened my phone and played music, humming along to a tune. When I felt the aircraft taxi away, I realised I had missed most of the safety announcement.

"In the event of an emergency over water, please place the vest over your head and pull to inflate. Your seat can also be used as a flotation device." The flight attendants continued, but my mind went blank, and I gripped my armrests tightly.

"Are you alright?" The man beside me asked in a Scottish accent. I forced myself to look at him, and nod.

"Nervous? It's okay. Many people are scared to fly."

"I'm not afraid of flying. More afraid of crashing into water."

"Ah" He nodded and smiled. "I'm Lachlan. I can't exactly say I'm afraid of water, but more what's in it. And I am a bit jumpy about flying".

The way he said water sent goosebumps up my arms.

"I'm Sahara, and I generally prefer to have my feet firmly in the desert sand." Lachlan laughed jovially. He was handsome, with long, dark, thick hair tied neatly into a bun. Beneath his long eyelashes sat big brown eyes. He had a surprisingly small nose, but it featured well with the facial hair that framed his chiselled jawline. He was well groomed and showed a hint of white whiskers peeking through his dark locks. It was flattering in a cute way. And the accent was working to calm my nerves.

"So, what made you decide to ride this pressurized tube of air out to an island surrounded by water?" He asked when they were airborne.

"Well, I was invited to the music symposium with my university. My choir and I are going to perform." I replied, smiling proudly.

"A choir! I haven't heard a choir in a very long time. I tend to avoid siren songs; I don't want to be lured to my death." I looked at him questioningly, my defenses up, though I wasn't sure why.

"Why did you call it a siren's song?" I asked.

"Where I come from, they tell stories of young women who seduce men with song to lure them into the depths of the ocean. The siren's call is unmistakably haunting, eerie, beautiful, irresistible – and deadly." he told her, smiling wide.

"If you have been invited to perform, I imagine your voices are beautiful and melodic, in fact talking to you now is quite hypnotic. I shall endeavour to see your performance."

"Are you performing?" She asked him.

"Good heavens, no! I am not one who is adept at music. I would rather listen and judge. I am an excellent judge of sounds, but I don't produce them quite as well." he barked a laugh as he sat back in his chair.

"I am traveling to be a judge for a competition of sorts. I have been away from home for far too long already, I am afraid." And he closed his eyes in thought, and then soon dozed off.

I sat in contemplation wondering how he could sleep so easily. I shook my head, and then turned my headphones back on, and brought up the piece I was composing. *Another minor key composition,* I thought. *It's always so eerie sounding.* I glanced at the man sleeping beside me, snoring loudly, like a walrus huffing and puffing. The flight attendant came by with water and snacks, and the man didn't wake until they were on final approach. He snorted awake and apologized for his noisy nap. We landed safely and exited the plane. While waiting for the bags, I snapped a selfie and sent it to dad.

"Made it safely to the island, Dad. Wish me luck!". Then followed my fellow choir mates out of the terminal and to the bus waiting outside. The humidity in the air made my hair limp as it stuck to my face. I had never felt humidity this thick. It hurt to breathe!

When we got to the hotel, we were given an itinerary for the symposium events and other attractions to check out on the island. We were supposed to perform our choir on day two. We had lots of time to spend exploring the sights.

But first, a good night's rest. I climbed into the queen size bed, and promptly passed out.

After a rather uneventful night I woke up for breakfast, starving. Good news, no nightmares. We had a list of speakers and performers and I wanted to catch a few. I met up with my professor and told her what I would be attending. She would attend some others and we could swap notes.

The others from our school were excited to see the volcanoes on the other island. It required a ferry and so

I turned it down. Could I get across the water on a boat? Nope, not happening.

I was chewing on a muffin when I entered the auditory hall and heard the most amazing voice. In all my years, I've never heard a male voice sound so alluring. The piece was something I had never heard, but it felt familiar.

As I approached the auditorium, he finished his melancholic song and I missed who was singing. I tried to check the itinerary, but there were no performances scheduled here this morning.

I chose a seat and sat down, looking for the voice I heard. If I ever started my own company, I'd want his voice.

I was surprised to see that the room was filling up. A young woman stepped out and began to talk about music. I listened with rapt attention, taking notes and being about as geeky as a music student could be. I spent the morning in that auditorium before heading out to the beach front to grab some lunch.

Sitting on the beach sand made me feel comforted, I was fond of sand. Dad often told me I would swim in sand instead of water if I could. I liked to remind him that I couldn't swim at all, but sand would be my pick. I love the graininess on my skin, the way it heats your feet from the soles. When you dig them in, the coolness takes over. Sand is like a non-Newtonian fluid. It can behave like both a solid and a liquid depending on the forces, and the composition.

This sand was decidedly wetter than my desert sand, it clung to my feet instead of slipping off, and it stuck to my hand. I mean, I had eaten sand plenty of times before, but nothing made me cringe more than sand in my mouth. Bleh. I listened to the waves as they came onto the shore. The sound was so foreign, but strangely enough, it was alluring. I wanted to go closer. I wanted to feel the ocean water. I shook my head. Imagine telling my dad I touched the ocean. I wondered if the airlines would let me take a jar, so that dad could remember the smell of the salty and humid fresh sea breeze.

I finished my lunch and returned to the hotel. There was a conference there this afternoon and I wanted to listen. It was about composing group pieces for different instruments. But I wanted to apply it to vocals.

Tomorrow my choir and I would perform, and I wanted to hear the group's opinions on vocal accompaniment, acapella, and symphonies.

It was an interesting afternoon; I asked a couple questions and got some baffled looks about intertwining vocals and harmonics to create something else. The group seemed puzzled but intrigued. I hope I can get my meaning across.

I met up with the choir for dinner and then a rehearsal. I had limited complaints. Chloe always sang off-key after eating, so that would be rectified in the morning. Josh was antsy and nervous and hit a couple of wobbles, but it sounded okay. I'd be happy with the performance.

Returning to my hotel room, I listened to the stories about a cavern on the other island. They spent a good part of the morning singing into it, and they wanted to explore the cave more. They showed me pictures and a recording of it, and it was great. Chloe was even in tune!

We went to our rooms, knowing the performance was priority for tomorrow. After that, they were free to drink, mingle and enjoy the island.

The performance was later today. As a group we met in the hotel for breakfast. We made sure Chloe didn't eat anything with dairy and had no coffee. I needed her on-key for this. While it wasn't a competition, we were going to perform a piece I wrote expressly for this group. It was my own composition, and while I don't like to boast, the group had insisted I write myself a part to sing.

We got to the auditorium where I met with the stage manager, and we went over the final touches. The beauty of my choir group is that we were almost acapella. The only instrument I included was a bamboo flute that Alice played for a brief period. Otherwise, it was all vocals.

With just six of us, it was almost not a choir. We had Josh and Jagmeet, whose voices were baritone and bass, they also did most of the baseline musical notes. Chloe was a rare alto, and even contralto when she wanted. Alice and Shaylene were my sopranos, and I fell into mezzo-soprano, but my vocal range could almost fill in the gaps between alto to contralto soprano. I spent a lot of time training my voice after I learned how to speak and talk, and then sing.

There was another group performing after us, but they were a symphonic choir, with an entire band. I aimed for us to sound like we had music accompaniment, with the most minimal number of instruments.

We were called onto the stage, and the six of us stood in a formation. I counted us in ,,, four, three, two, ahhhhh. The echo in the auditorium was beautiful. It was perfect. Chloe was on key and Josh held his notes. The room was dead silent when we finished. As the final note rang out across the room. Alice leaned forward and whispered, "I think we entranced them again, you and your siren voice." I chuckled and the spell was broken. Then the applause started. I noticed a woman in the back, in a green and purple dress who wasn't clapping. She turned and walked out. We took our bows and were led off the stage. We watched the other group. The woman in purple caught my attention, and I leaned over to Alice and whispered "Did you see the lady at the back by the door? She was dressed in purple, and just nodded along, before rushing out."

Alice shook her head "No, I wasn't looking at the back of the room, too many faces were staring at us. We were awesome!" "Yeah, we were!" We watched the next performance, and then the discussions began. They asked me questions about how I made the sounds blend so well to be almost like one haunting voice. Chloe piped up and spoke, "She's the Siren of the Desert!" My face turned a deep crimson as the other artists agreed with her. "Her voice is so ethereal."

"It's like magic"

"I've never heard anything so hauntingly beautiful." Someone called, "Let's hear her sing again!"

I didn't think I could turn a deeper shade of red, but there it was. I was proud, but so embarrassed. Alice and Chloe dragged me up, Shaylene, Josh and Jagmeet clapping and encouraging me.

"B-But what do I sing?" I asked the audience.

"Sing a sea song!" came a male voice, "I bet she'd sound like a real siren!"

Chloe leaned over and whispered, "Sing a lullaby, watch them become putty." I nodded. It was a good way to use the echo in the room and showcase the range of my voice.

Hush, little baby, don't you cry,
I will sing you a lullaby,
Dream of things that are dry as sand,
Keep your feet forever on land.
Hush, little baby, remember me,
There are dangers lurking in the sea.
When the moon is high and the tide is strong,
Stay away and remember my song.
Close your eyes and get some sleep,
And in my heart you'll forever be.

I finished the song and looked around. The audience was staring at me, some with mouths open, some had closed their eyes and placed their hands on their hearts. I coughed a little, and Alice whispered, "Those were some weird lyrics, but I liked it." I looked at her as the audience stood up, clapping away.

The stage lead came and guided us backstage.

"You need to meet Araxie. She's a vocal teacher on the next island over. She would love your voice, even if just to show her students what they can achieve." He handed me a business card, **Araxie's Vocal School for Singers**, it read. There was an address, but no number, or email

"Is there another way to reach out to her?" I asked him, knowing I couldn't get to the next island.

"No, everyone must go to her home and sing to enter. Only those with voices she deems worthy can enter the door. She's produced the best vocalists ever." I smiled, thanked him and left. Alice piped up beside me "Can we go? Please?" I smiled sadly at her."You guys are all welcome to go, but I unfortunately will not be going with you. I can't cross to the other islands." "You definitely can cross, it's just a short ferry ride. We can keep you in the middle, so that you can't see the water. We can even blindfold you." "No, Alice, I can't go. It would be extremely embarrassing to be seen shrieking bloody murder off the top of the ferry before it even gets going. I–I can't do it. But I encourage you to go see her!" We met up with the rest of the group and filed out of the auditorium, but before I left, I heard that same male voice, bellowing through the auditorium. I looked up to see the stagehand, singing his heart out. I had goosebumps on my skin. I walked up to meet him. He stopped singing when he saw me and smiled. "I really think you should go see Araxie. Your voice is exactly what she is looking for. She taught me to sing. She also gave me the legs to stand on, so to speak." I smiled back and shook my head. "I can't leave this island unless it's by plane. There is no way I will be leaving the ground for water. Sorry, I am terrified of water. It's a miracle I even came to this island." "You are terrified of water?" He asked, raising his eyebrow. "That's quite a feat for someone who can sing so well that people call her a mermaid!""They call me the desert siren. I wish I could swim in the sand to prove I really was a mermaid." He tilted his head and smirked. "Do you know the difference between a mermaid and a siren?" He asked."I'm not exactly up to date with marine life, let alone sea myths. My knowledge is through movies like *The Little Mermaid.* He smiled, and sat on the edge of the stage, motioning for me to follow.

"Well, only women can be sirens, and they have given up their souls to the sea. In exchange, they must do the bidding of the Sea herself. Mermaids can be male or female, and are born in the sea, not *of* the sea. Merfolk are the usual half-human with a tail. They look the same above the water as below. Sirens only look like women above the water. Below the surface, they are scaly and scabby, and it's not really a tail, but their legs stick together and act like a tail. Both merfolk and sirens can sing beautifully, but a siren has a gift from the Sea that makes her voice so enchanting that it will force a man to dive into the ocean. The siren will drag them down into the abyss. A mermaid lives and breathes and has no bonds to the ocean. If they want to walk on land they can, but a siren must stay in the sea until her service is complete, then she can re-join the land." He laughed. "You can't possibly be a siren, love, a mermaid perhaps, but with a fear of water, I'm pretty sure you just have a beautiful voice. I'll try to get a message to Araxie to come listen. Although, I think she was here briefly. Hard to tell with her, she's a bit aloof." He stood up to leave the auditorium, checking his cell phone.

I smiled. "By the way, I'm Sahara, and you are?" and I reached out for his hand. "I'm Kai, I work part time up here, and sometimes elsewhere."

Kai, I thought, is an interesting guy.

I met the choir for dinner at a nearby restaurant. The girls were planning to go clubbing tonight, and Josh and Jag wanted to go to the casino. They tried to convince me to join them, but I felt no desire to dress up in the skimpiest outfit I owned to dance the night away. I had other things in mind.

After dinner, I put on a long white light linen dress, my crossbody purse, matching flip flops and went down to the boardwalk. I gave the sea a wide berth, but the wind was cool and blowing in the salt, and it certainly felt different from the desert. The ocean waved at me from the beach, beckoning. I was tempted, but fear paralyzed me and kept me far away.

The boardwalk itself was teeming with people, popping in and out of gift shops, coffee shops and local artisanal shops that lined the way. I wandered into a couple and had a look. I wanted to bring back something from the ocean for my dad. A small bottle with sand and water caught my eye. It was perfect! He had been a sailor and fisherman in his youth. I was sure he would be okay with the bottle. I tucked it into my purse and kept strolling down the boardwalk.

A cute little ice cream shop caught my eye, and I wandered in. *58 flavours* the sign read. It had the usuals: chocolate, vanilla, rainbow sorbet, but there were also a couple that intrigued me. Salt-Water Taffy Flavour. Sea-Weed Flavour. Jellyfish Flavour? So strange. "Ah, the desert siren! Care to try an ice cream from the sea to see if you can be swayed to like water?" I turned to find Kai's dark curly locks dripping wet as he waltzed in with no shirt on, bright coloured Hawaiian flower tattoos adorning his chest. Shorts and flip flops on his wet feet, squeaking when he walked.

"I think I'll stick with something more traditional, thank you." I responded.

"Kai! I've told you before to stay outside when you're still wet!" The woman behind the counter shrieked at him. He just smirked and continued to the counter.

"Give me two scoops of Jellyfish flavour please!"

"Fine, fine, but get out of the store or I will make you mop it up!" She yelled back, shooing him out.

"Sorry about that, he's a local pain in the ass. What can I get for you?" She smiled warmly. Her dark hair was tied into a bun on top of her head. "Give her the seaweed flavour, Namiko" Kai yelled from the doorway.

"GET OUT!" She yelled.

"I am outside."

"Then stop pestering my customers." She looked back at me, her almond shaped eyes a striking sparkling blue.

"Sorry, darling, the man doesn't understand boundaries." "Can I get a single scoop of mocha, please?"

"You sure can! How are you enjoying the visit to the island? If you've run into Kai already, you must have been at the auditorium?" She picked up a sugar cone and scooped a very large scoop of the brown ice cream with chunks of chocolate in it.

"Uh- yeah, I have been at the auditorium. I'm enjoying the visit so far. I wish there were more attractions on this island."

"Oh! Why not travel to the other island nearby? The ferries are all free of charge, and the rides are quite short."

"I can't get on the ferries. It's flights only. Anything neat nearby?" She looked thoughtful as she handed me my cone.

"I suppose there is Echo Cavern, but it's a bit of a hike. Locals like to go up there and sing and shout and just be merry." "Oh, that actually sounds really cool." I smiled as I started to eat my cone, watching as she placed a double scoop of teal-coloured ice cream into a cone.

"Come with me for a second," She beckoned me to follow. "Here's your jellyfish ice cream, Kai."

"Thanks, Namiko," He dove right into it. "TH-AH-RA, wath'sup?"

"For god's sake, don't talk with your mouth full," Namiko told him and smacked him upside the head. "She was asking about local attractions on *this* island, and the only thing I could think of was Echo Cavern. Think you would want to lead the way?" He stopped mid-lick on his cone and smiled widely.

"Yethhh.." He swallowed. "Your voice would sound amazing there! Let's go!"

I smiled, "Right now?" I asked.

"Er, Nam, when are you done with your shift?"

"I'm done at 6:30, my relief should be here in ten minutes though, and Melody is my ride tonight."

"Will Melody want to come?" Kai asked Namiko.

"Of course, she'll want to come, she hardly ever gets away from Araxia's manor on the other island. Text her and let her know. We should get there around seven thirty, and the sunset is around ten here, so we have lots of time." Kai pulled out his cellphone and started to type one-handed. Pretty impressive.

I sat quietly eating my mocha ice cream and taking in the sights. I pulled out my phone and texted Alice.

'Hope you're having fun. I'm going to a local place called Echo Cavern with Kai, the stagehand from the auditorium this morning, and a couple of his friends." Better to give out information and be safe, than to go with random strangers into an unknown local cave. I put my phone back in my bag and sat with Kai.

"You thur you don wanna twy the delifith ithe cweam?" he asked with a full mouth. I burst out laughing. "Is it made from actual jellyfish?" I joked.

"Yeah, it is. It even glows in the dark. It's super tasty too, salty, and sweet." My mouth twisted in disgust, and I shook my head. "Nope, no thank you. I am good with my mocha ice cream," and then I bit into the cone. "Ahh, too bad." He then stuck the whole cone in his mouth and chewed. I burst out laughing again, "You look like a chipmunk!"

"Whath's a thipmunk?" He asked, a puzzled look on his face. I opened my phone and googled a picture, one where the cheeks were puffed out and showed Kai. He burst out laughing, spewing some cone on the ground. Namiko came out and waved to a very pale girl with long flowing red hair.

"Melody, over here." The new girl walked up and sat down beside Kai and flicked his nose.

"Hullo, Kai, long time no see." She had an Irish accent, which kind of surprised me. I looked at my three new friends and their dynamics. Kai was chill, calm and cool, basically a surfer dude.

"Melody, this is Sahara. She sings better than you do." Kai told her, smiling.

"Wait, don't tell her that. She'll get worried about her place at Araxie's school." Namiko said.

"Nice to meet you, Sahara," Melody said, extending her hand. "If these two hadn't made it clear, I go to school on the other island, with Ms Araxie." "Nice to meet you too. I'm from Arizona. Kai told me to go see her." "She was on this island today. Picking up her regularly scheduled shipments." Melody shrugged. "That's why we have the day off."

"Ah well, more time together. Let's head off to the cave." Kai leapt up, leading the way from the ice cream shoppe. The three of us followed, all in flip flops. Kai had found a Hawaiian shirt and pulled it on, unbuttoned. They started down the beach, chatting and bantering.

Melody was talking about the vocal training she was undergoing, and how Araxie was a great help at extending range and capabilities.

It's always the same songs though. Like she doesn't like any other songs. It's kind of strange. I mean, the songs are hard, and they do stretch my capabilities, but it would be nice to sing something different."

"Can you sing something else for practice? By your-self?" Namiko asked Melody

"Oh gosh, no. If she hears anything different, she gets crazy. We can't 'misuse our voices' is how she puts it."

We were steadily climbing upwards on a rocky trail. There was a small path that was worn into the rock, but it didn't look too used. The palm trees were still growing ever higher towards the sky, and the scent mixed with the salty sea water. I was starting to long for my sandy beach when Melody pointed to a fork in the path. "Left or right?" She asked the group."Left leads down towards the ocean path, and the bottom. But right leads to the top of the huge cavern, where the echo is the best." Namiko explained

"Obviously right," Kai said, heading upwards. "We want the best view, and the best echoes."

The three of us followed Kai up the narrow path, and when I looked over the side, I found a breath-taking view of the island.

"Beautiful, isn't it?" Namiko asked, looking out toward the ocean. I smiled and pointed down to the island. "I'm more interested in the land view; since I prefer to keep my feet on land." "Come here" Kai sang to the cliffside, and I heard his echo reverberate through the cliffside.We were now atop the very highest point of the island, but there was a cavern at the top. It was dark smooth rock, and you could hear the ocean lapping at the bottom of the drop.

"It's about one hundred fifty feet down, and it's a straight plunge into the ocean." Melody said.

"It's not usually deadly, but still pretty scary. Even for those of us on the island." Kai said as he sat on the ledge and swung his feet over. Namiko joined beside him on the ledge, and called out

"Hello Ocean! I miss you!" her voice echoed and echoed, growing fainter and fainter.

"Melody, sing us a song?" Namiko asked as I tentatively sat near the edge. I wasn't going to swing my legs over though, that ocean below was far too scary. Melody nodded.

She began to sing a folk song that I recognised as 'Jolly Sailor Bold,' but the sound of her voice was amazing. She was very talented; the echo of the cavern below made it eerie and haunting.

My heart is pierced by Cupid
I disdain all glittering gold
There is nothing can console me
But my jolly sailor bold

When she finished, there was silence among the four of us as we sat there. Her voice had enchanted us all, but then Kai yelled into the cavern. "Take that, Sea-Witch!

Beautiful voices that aren't sirens!" I looked at him, confused, and Namiko elbowed him hard.

"Ow, Nam, that hurt." "You don't want the wrath of the sea-witch on you, do you?" *The sea-witch? Sirens?* I thought. Melody interrupted me. "Kai said you can sing really well too. Let's hear!" she said.

"Yeah, let's hear something fun." Kai said.

Are you going to Scarborough Fair?Parsley, sage, rosemary and thyme. Remember me to one who lived there. She once was a true love of mine.

Have her make me a cambric shirt. Parsley, sage, rosemary and thyme. Without no seams, nor fine needle work. Then she'll be a true love of mine.

I stopped and the three of them were staring at me, jaws open.

"What?" I asked embarrassed. "Was it off key? I'm sorry." I stood up and started to walk away. Melody was the first to get up and chase me, "Wait, Sahara." I stopped and turned around to look at them.

"I heard you sing that lullaby earlier today, and thought your voice was ethereal and amazing. But up here, it rendered us speechless. And it's hard for a voice to do that. Are you sure you're human?" Kai said, winking and patting the spot beside him.

"As far as I know. I've lived my entire life in the desert." "Let's keep singing! We'll make the sea witch go crazy!" Namiko smacked him again, but I returned and sat with them.

Kai started this time with "Hoist the Colours." Melody laughed, and joined in, and so did Namiko.

"*Heave ho, thieves and beggars, never shall we die*"

I sang along with them until the sun began to set. I was entranced by the harmonics the echo cavern created. It was so amazing, and so beautiful. I focused intently on the echoes, and so I didn't hear the person move behind me. I didn't even feel the push, but the next thing I knew, I was falling. My voice caught in my throat, and I tried to scream, but nothing would come out! I kept falling, and falling, and then I felt a painful sting as I hit the water. I blacked out.

I was underwater. The sensation was so foreign as I gasped for air and immediately swallowed the ocean water. I tried to cough, but the air escaped in a bubble and water surrounded me. I thrashed in the water, trying to find my way up, my legs started to stick together, tangled in my dress. I began kicking them harder, searching for the surface. The cough turned into a gasp, and I felt a strange watery sensation along my neck, but

I wasn't hurting for air. I think I was breathing water. *What the hell*? I tried to calm myself to figure out which way was up, but I couldn't find it. I tried to kick, but I couldn't separate my legs. I tried to look down at my body, but it was dark and I couldn't see at all. My hands started to feel like they were moving more water, more surface. I used one hand to feel the other and felt a weird rubbery material between my fingers.

Suddenly, the water calmed, and I was able to figure out that I was, in fact, breathing the ocean water. I could feel the water flow in and out through my neck. I was floating in the water. Another new sensation, I've never floated before. I was weightless, but my legs were stuck together. I could feel that they were separate. *What was this? Why am I in the water?* I heard something below me and tried to look down and saw nothing but darkness. It was lighter above me, and I tried to propel myself upward.

I broke the surface and attempted to see which direction to go. There was nothing around and the sun had begun to set. I didn't know how to swim, so I panicked. A wave rose and dumped over me, pushing me back underwater. I gasped again, swallowing a ton of salted water, but again, I was able to breathe. My eyes widened and I tried to focus my eyes on seeing something. There had to be land somewhere. I couldn't die in the ocean. Dad would freak. Losing his wife and his daughter to the sea would be devastating.

I pumped my legs and discovered that if I pumped my legs a certain way, I could move forward quite a bit. If I moved my hands with my legs, I was propelling forward even further. I tried to make my eyes see something, and then I heard a small click and there was a yellow glow. I could see something swimming in the distance. I opened my mouth and the salt water rushed in, filling my mouth and lungs, but I screamed anyway.

"HEEELP ME" Bubbles flowed out, but I could hear my voice echoing in the water. *How the hell?* I screamed again "HELP ME! PLEASE SOMEONE HELP ME!"The figure swimming in the distance was growing larger in my eyes. It was a walrus or a seal, or some large sea animal. It looked like a grey blob with a green glow about him. He swam up to me and I shuddered. "Help me to land, please?" I sobbed to the walrus and reached for him.

"To the land, are you sure?" asked the creature, in a familiar Scottish accent.

"Yes, land. I can't swim, I'm going to die." The creature managed a bark, and I thought it was a laugh, but I moved nearer to him anyway. "Alright, lass, follow me then."

"I don't know how to swim." I sobbed. Wait, why was I talking to this creature? How was it understanding me? Never mind, just as long as I could find land, I would sort it out later. "You can't swim? You're doing a dang good job of it." The walrus laughed at me again. "Oh well, grab on, I'll take you to the nearest island." I latched on, and he swam away fast, dragging my body with him.

His skin was smooth, and he glided through the water with ease, even with my weight dragging behind him. He came out of the depths of the ocean, and we broke the surface. I gasped as the air hit my lungs and I started to cough up the water. I could see a beach ahead and urged him forward,

"L-land" I sputtered out, gasping the humid ocean air.

"You're sure, lass? You are a creature of the water; you will dry up on land." Nevertheless, he moved close to the beach, and I dragged myself out of the water onto the sand. The sand shifted around me and wrapped me in what felt like a warm embrace. The sun was nearly set, casting a red glow around everything. I lay in the sand, gasping and trying to sort out my body. Suddenly remembering the water and the sensation around my neck, I reached for it, trying to feel for the gills I swore were there. My neck felt smooth and normal. Then I looked down at my legs, tangled in my dress, and I was able to separate them from each other. *The dress is what caused them to stick together,* I thought. But my legs and feet were a reddish colour that they weren't before. I looked at my hands, they were also reddish and there was a webbing that was shrinking away between each of my fingers. I shook my hand, trying to dislodge the goop in them until they felt normal. I rolled onto my side and rocked onto my knees, trying to push myself to stand up. I needed to get away from the water.

The seal galumphed onto the beach, watching me curiously. I pushed off and stood.

"How did you do that?" He asked. I turned and looked at the creature who saved me, and before I let the confusion take over. I needed to make sense of this situation.

"Thank you, Mr. Seal. I don't think I would have survived without you. But now I must figure out where I am, and what the fuck just happened."

"Oi, sailor's language, lass! What'd you mean 'you wouldn't have survived'? You're a sea creature, like I am." I looked back at him and realised I was talking to a seal.

"I must've hit my head pretty good or swallowed too much water. Seals don't talk and I can't swim."

But here I am, I thought. "What the actual fucking hell just happened?" I shouted. "I was on the edge of that echoing cavern, singing, then I was falling, and then, and then... I was in the water. The cavern, where's the cavern?" I looked around for any other sight of land, but there was nothing. "And then I was swept away, being pulled along, but I tried to breathe, and something happened to my neck." I reached for my neck again, almost clawing at it. "I shouldn't be able to breathe underwater" I shouted again. "I've spent my entire life in the desert avoiding water. What the actual fuck?" I turned to look at the seal, who was still just staring at me, head tilted. "I remember reaching the surface and not being able to breathe air. Then I was back underwater, and I ... I screamed. And you.." I turned and pointed at the seal" YOU came when I screamed. Sound doesn't travel that far underwater. It can't. And then you talked to me, which is also impossible. Seals don't talk." I was looking at the water again, and my legs.

"My legs were stuck together, and something covered my eyes, and I could see, and breathe underwater." I sat down in the sand, feeling the soft ground beneath me, and looked at my hands again. "Why was my skin red, and was there webbing between my fingers? And why were my legs stuck together, and WHAT IN THE HELL ARE YOU DOING?!" I shouted as the seal pulled his head back, and a human came out from beneath it. I stared in horror as a naked man stepped out, folded the sealskin, and placed it beside him on the beach. I backed away and turned my head, not comprehending what was going on.

"Calm down, lass. You are okay. You're on land, you're safe from the water." The man/seal thing said to me. I looked back at him, and he knelt in front of meHe was totally naked from head to toe, his skin was a dark tanned colour, and it glistened in the last light of the setting sun. His long hair was a greyish black, like the seal he had been. There were a few white whiskers in his goatee, and they twitched when he talked.

"My name is Lachlan. What is yours?" He asked, speaking slowly and calmly. I searched my mind to remember where I had heard that name before but came up blank.

"I'm Sahara."

"The girl from the plane! Well, this is unexpected." He exclaimed. I looked back at him, and yes, it was the man from the plane, who snored loudly the whole way.

"Well, Sahara, welcome to what the merfolk call Echo Island."

"Merfolk?" I asked, confused as hell. How was this man able to swim as a seal? Where the hell was I, and why was he talking about merfolk? My head was dizzy with a hundred questions. "Ah yes, Mermaids are real. So are sirens, and other mythical creatures of the sea. Do you know all the folk tales? Well, they are generally true. Come, walk with me, we will get you to the shelter on the island here for the night." He stood up and offered his hand to help me up.

I hesitated at his outstretched hand and looked back out to the water.

"Can you walk, or should I pick you up and carry you?" he asked. I just stared straight ahead, still trying to process what he said. The sun had settled below the horizon and the last bits of purple were fading. I started to shiver. He dropped the folded seal skin in my lap. He bent down, placing one are under my knees and one behind my back, lifting me until I was being carried.

"Hey, I can walk!" I protested, but I really wasn't sure I could. "Shh, just relax. You are in shock. I will get you to the shelter. I've never met a siren like you." He walked quickly inland, between the palm trees. I relaxed against his warm chest and sleep quickly washed over me.

I opened my eyes, and they were glowing. I was floating, surrounded by water. The water was black, but
I could see. I wriggled my legs, but they were stuck together again. This time I looked down. My dress wasn't
tangled but flowing freely in the water. My legs wouldn't
separate. I lifted the dress to try and see what had bound
them, but then realised my feet were missing. Well not
missing, but in their place, connected to each other was

a red flappy thing. It looked like a fish tail. I tried to wiggle my toes, tried to feel for them, but instead the tail twitched. It swished and I felt the water flow over the tip. I opened my mouth to scream, and it filled with salty water. I gurgled, trying to force the water out, coughing and sputtering, flailing in the water. *"HELP ME"*, I screamed.

"Calm down, Sahara" a voice said, and I opened my eyes. Above me stood a tall man with dark hair and brown-black eyes. His nose twitched when I kept staring and the short whiskers on his upper lip were pulled into a small smile.

"You're okay." He said, a deep rumbling sound in his chest.

I tried to focus on where I was, but my eyes were drawn to this man. He had on a pair of blue-grey shorts that hung loosely from his hips. *Damn. My dreams are getting weirder.* I tried to sit up and found my legs were tangled in a blue blanket.

I was lying on a cot made up of some lightweight wood and palm tree leaves, lashed and woven together.

I untangled my legs, relieved I was still in my maxi dress and had undergarments on.

"Um, Hi?" I asked tentatively.

"It's Lachlan, lass". *Right. I knew that.*

"Lachlan," I said, testing the name in my mouth.

"Um. I appear to have either died and gone to heaven, hit my head something awful, or I'm just straight-up hallucinating. So, if you're a hallucination, please tell me, so I can go back to what I was doing before." I sighed and looked around the space.

It appears to be a half-shelter, lean-to thing. A makeshift area to block out the rain or sun. It was made up of palm trees and their leaves were woven together to make screens. It appeared as if the screens were able to shift from position to position to keep the wind or water out from whichever direction. There were some extra screens lying beside the last one standing. They were made to snap together and even hung down to form a make-shift roof.

The sun was setting just under the horizon, the sky beginning to turn pink.

"What's the last thing you recall, lass?" He spoke but followed my eyes to the rising sun.

"I... I remember the sun setting. And floating in water. And red. I was red. Why was I red?!" My voice hitched and panic started to flood through my veins, making my voice rise. Suddenly I felt his arms around my body, warm and strong, holding me in place.

"It's okay, lass, no need to panic here. Tell me what else you remember."

I breathed his scent, it was musky, and salty, like the ocean, but also like a breeze of fresh air. He still held my back to his chest, holding his arms across my own and keeping me in place.

I stared at the sunrise; the pink was turning orange now.

"I was in the water. I screamed and called for help. I could breathe underwater?" I questioned, trying to tilt my head to look at him. His arms held me firm.

"Aye, you can breathe underwater." I felt his head nod.

"How is that possible?" I whispered to myself.

He chose this moment to release me, and I immediately felt cold from the loss of his body heat.

"Do you accept that you can breathe underwater?" He asked me when I turned to look at him. He had a serious expression on his face. This was no joke. Was he tricking me?

"I think so. I don't know?" was my half-hearted response. I saw him glance at the sky, taking on a yellow morning glow.

"You're going to be alright, Sahara. Trust your instincts like you did in the water. See if you can piece the puzzle together. Don't wander too far. There's some food in one of the containers." He pointed at a pile that looked like screens, but on closer inspection, there was a woven basket with a lid.

"I'll be back this evening before sundown. I promise to give you answers, slow and steady."

"You're, you're leaving me here?!" The panic was obvious in my voice, but I didn't care.

"I've got to be somewhere for a special event, and they would have my skin if I didn't show."

And with that he grabbed the spotted coat that was folded neatly at the foot of the cot.

"I'll be back, Sahara. Don't cause too much trouble" He winked and walked away.

I wanted to chase after him, but my legs were still shaky and that feeling of being stuck together filtered up into my mind.

What happened to me? I asked. I went to the basket to find it was filled with water and freshly caught fish.

Guess I will need to make a fire to cook these. I started to pilfer through the nets and baskets and other items strewn haphazardly throughout the makeshift camp-site. I found an apple and gave up on looking for fire and just sat and ate and stared at the beach and the lapping water. Mocking me.

Did I really breathe underwater?

Did my skin really web and turn red?

Where the hell am I?

And that last one hit me with a start. That should have been my first damned question to Lachlan. Where am I, and how do I get home? Maybe he's getting a rescue?

Maybe he's left me here to die.

Fuck, Sahara. You're so stupid. He isn't even real. He was a seal. A seal that came to your rescue when you called him underwater.

I must be dead. But then, why is this apple so good and yet, not as sweet as it should be?

I walked to the edge of the little camp hut looking for my shoes and realised I probably lost them in the water. I kicked the sand in anger at my own stupidity. Was I really trapped on this island? Is there any way to make a call?

Suddenly it dawned on me. My purse. Where was my bag? It was a crossbody and should have stuck to me. My phone was there, I could call for help. I could turn on the GPS tracking signal and hope that the choir would be looking for me.

Oh my God. Chloe, Alice, Josh, Jagmeet and Shaylene. Were they looking for me, as panicked as I was? Do they have search and rescue? Is there a way for them to find me?

I remember sitting at the ledge of Echo Cavern singing with those three friends. Kai, Namiko and Melody. I was sitting with them and then I was falling. But I don't remember feeling anyone push me.

I screamed, but so did they. I heard Kai call my name as I fell, but no one raced after me. Did they think I died? How did I end up in open water near a seal? How did the seal understand me, and I understood him?

Wait ... did the seal become human? No. No. There was no way. That's not possible. I stood and paced the beach barefoot, my white dress flowing in the breeze. It can't be real. I'm delusional. I pinched myself.

Ow. That hurt! OK. Not dreaming. Not delusional. So that leaves real. This is actually happening to me.

Can I breathe underwater? And if I can, why the hell am I so terrified of it. Shouldn't I love water? Shouldn't I want to be *in* the water? Ugh. I had a headache. Where's the ibuprofen when you need it?

"Where's my purse, Lachlan?!" I screamed to the ocean out of spite. "Where's my shoes? Huh?" Abandoned on this island with nothing but the clothes on my back. I kicked the sand again and a crab waved at me. I shrieked.

"Ahh. Dammit. You scared me" I told the skittering crab. It wandered off into the beach waters.

"Sorry!" I called after it. I liked hearing my voice in the open air. It wasn't echoing like the cavern, but it had an open carrying air around it.

"*Sweet dreams are made of these. Who am I to disagree*" I sang out loud to nothing.

"*Travel the world and the seven Seas. Everybody's looking for something.*" Such a strange song to come to mind, but it was distracting me. And I didn't notice the tide was rising and my feet were getting wet.

"*Some of them want to use you.*" I paused when I sang this line and looked down. There was a splash in the water.

I stood still and watched as a school of fish swam up and stopped in the shallowest water they could. I took a step back. This was weird, right?

Behind me was the skittish crab from earlier. And he brought friends.

What's going on? They stood around me, staring and being still. The fish in the water were just staying in place. I lifted my dress and ran back to the shelter, huddling up on the cot and grasped my knees to my chest.

This isn't real. I'm crazy. I'm totally hallucinating.

I rocked back and forth on the cot for a while. Willing something to change; to shimmer to prove I'm in a fantasy world. I hit my head and died. This is the weirdest form of hell they could pick for me. I must have fallen asleep again, because I awoke to the smell of a campfire, and the sun had again set.

"Ah, you're alright, lass. Have you pieced anything together?" The flames flashed shadows across his face, and his jaw line looked much more defined, more chiseled than I remembered. He was sitting cross-legged on the sand, the grey shorts that hung loosely on his hips not hiding his muscled legs.

"You're back?" I looked out and saw the sun was low in the sky, but not quite setting. It was evening, so I had slept most of the day away.

"Aye, I said I'd be back. Have you eaten anything?" His eyes flashed with concern.

"I ... I had an apple?"

"Is that all?!" His eyes lit up and he frowned.

"No wonder you haven't digested anything, you've not eaten. Sit down on the sand beside the fire." He stood up and went to rummage through the bins. He opened the one with fish and promptly stabbed one with a sharp stick nearby. I winced at the show of violence, but my stomach rumbled anyway.

I stared into the flames, still unable to comprehend exactly what was going on here.

Was Lachlan my captor? I thought? But he seems like a nice guy. *Maybe it's the accent.*

He returned and handed me another apple and stuck the fish into the fire.

His nose bunched up when the smell overwhelmed the place.

"You do prefer it cooked, right?" He asked, cocking his head to the side.

"Phwat kin ov qestin if dat?" I asked, my mouth full of apple. I covered my mouth and giggled as I tried to swallow. He just shrugged and went back to monitoring the cooking fish.

"Aye lass. Have you gone into the water?"

My face blanched and I stopped mid bite.

The water.

"No. Why would I go into the water?" He sighed and his nose twitched.

"You really haven't pieced together what you are?" He held out the stick of cooked fish. I looked at the fish, then back at him and tried to figure out what he was saying.

"Take it. Eat." He pushed the stick into my hand and walked around the fire. He dropped down onto the sand, his back against the screen.

He seemed to be fighting an internal battle.

"Is something wrong?" I asked, suddenly not hungry.

"No, Lass. Just thinking. You really have no idea about who or what you are, and I don't want to break your mind further than it seems to be." He looked up from under his eyelids.

"Eat." He grumbled. I pulled a piece of the fish off and ate it. It was so good. I moaned a little and I swear I saw him smirk.

"Okay, so out with it. Whatever you are trying to claim is going to break my brain. Or whoever or whatever you think I am. Just spit it out." I tore at the fish and kept eating.

"Because when I was near the beach, a school of fish swam up to me. And the crabs all stood in a line like they were expecting something from me."

"The sea creatures come to the sound of your voice." He said simply. "I too was drawn to your voice, your call."

"Yes, you were in the water. But a seal came to me. Not you. And while you have some similarities, you are clearly human like me."

He barked a laugh, and it sounded just like a seal. My eyes widened, as he shook with barking laughter. It was shocking, and cute in a weird way. He looked like a shaking puppy.

"You think I'm human? You're not even human!" He roared with laughter. I stopped.

"What?" I looked at my hands, picturing the red hue and the webbing. The sensation of breathing underwater.

I'm not human? How was that possible?

"No, No, I'm human. " I shook my head.

"Would you like to see what you are?" He asked quietly. He stood up and took my hand, leading me to the beach.

"For someone who has no idea, this is going to be a huge shock." He spoke calmly, talking in hushed tones, like I was a child.

Put your feet into the water, up to your calves."

I... I can't go in the water." I stammered as my fear paralyzed me.

He blinked in confusion, then his face brightened in the setting sun.

"Are you – are you afraid of water?" He asked quietly.

I swallowed and nodded yes. *How humiliating, I thought.*

"Oh Sahara. I'm so sorry," *There it is. The pity. A girl who is afraid of water."* Let's get back to the fire. We can do this slowly. "

"Have you seen my purse?" I asked. "It had my phone in it, and if there's reception, I can text my dad and my choir and let them know I'm safe and haven't drowned."

He shook his head. "I didn't see a bag with you."

"Do you have a phone?" I asked suddenly. He smiled and turned in a circle. "And where would I keep it?"

"What about that coat you keep close?" I asked. He smiled and went and picked it up.

"This isn't exactly a coat, Lass." He handed it to me. It was soft, and smooth, with a fine fur on the outside. A dark blueish brown and spotted, it looked a little like a hide. I tried to open it and shake it out, and he barked his laugh again.

"Sahara, darling. That's my skin."

"W hat?!" I dropped the coat onto the sand. I quickly reached down to pick it up again and looked back at him. Something flashed from memory, an old folktale, a myth about humans who could wear the skin of an animal and become them. What were they called? '

"I'm a Selkie, lass, from Scotland. I am a seal, who can shift into a human." He smiled, as he swung his coat over his shoulders, and then buttoned it up. I was mesmerized by the swift transformation, where a man, a gorgeous man, once stood, was now a cute grey seal, with twitching whiskers.

"And you, if you can understand me, are a very unusual version of a siren."

A siren. How could I be a siren, I let my mind spiral, struggling to understand. Sirens were water creatures. I was anything but that. My brain refused to believe anything he said, despite witnessing it. Lachlan moved us back to the campfire, and simply let me sit quietly, while skewering fish to cook. I remember staring into the flames, digging my toes into the sand as the sun sank below the horizon.

My heart was hammering in my chest, and I was breathing heavily.

"Are you alright?" The voice came from behind me. I nearly jumped out of my skin and screamed.

"Shh, calm down, It's me, Lachlan." I tried to see, but it was just dark. Then I felt his warm hand reach out and hold mine.

"Whatever has you spooked, you're safe with me." The whispered voice helped to calm me down. Then my brain tried to catch up.

I'm on a beach, a deserted island, with a man who saved me, who was somehow also a seal, I might not be human, and...

I felt his hand brush against my cheek, his finger wiping away the tears I hadn't known were falling.

"It's alright. darling. I know it's a lot to take in, to try and understand. I'll sit with you all night."

I moved over and patted the cot next to me.

"Just ... hold me?" I whispered. "I just need to be grounded, and even though you aren't real, I can at least feel you, and know that you are there."

"Aye, I can do that, lass."

I sank onto the sand and sat cross-legged beside him, my head leaning against his shoulder. He stayed quiet, letting me rest against him. My dreams faded from memory, and I was feeling sleepy again.

I woke up, wrapped in his arms, my head across his chest and we were both lying in the sand. He was snoring, a light snore, but he still held me tight. I rose up to see him in the pre-dawn light, but when I moved, his hands tightened around my waist.

I froze, my heartbeat racing as he squeezed me gently to his warm chest.

"Are you trying to sneak away?" he asked, the sleep making his voice gravelly.

"No, I, I." He released me from his embrace, and I used my hands to prop myself up, feeling suddenly alone and cold.

I was looking down at him now, my hair hanging in waves around my face, my hands on his chest holding me up. My cheeks flushed as I realised my position, but he lifted his right hand and cupped my warm cheek.

"No tears, lass. You can come or go, stay in my arms, or run for the sea, but if you need me, just call and I will protect you" He lifted his hand and tucked my loose hair behind my ear.

What he said released some of the tension I was feeling, and I dropped my head back onto his chest, and hugged him back.

"You're going to need a hair tie for that". He commented absently, before tucking his arm under his head.

"You're an interesting one, lass. I'd like to know more about you."

"What do you want to know?" My voice was shaky. "I'm not really anything special. A nobody from the middle of the desert of nothing."

He laughed, and I could feel the sound reverberating in my chest and I relaxed into it. His other hand had found my upper back and just lightly placed it on me, not holding me down, but securing me from rolling into the sand.

"You're not 'nobody'. You've caught my eye, several times now. And now that my interest is piqued, I need satisfying answers."

"You need satisfying?" I asked as the grey of the morning started to shift to colour.

He looked me in the eye and smirked. My face flushed, and I looked down, mortified.

"You need satisfying answers?" I tried to correct my words.

"I'll take whatever you give me." And he pulled my chin up to look him in the eye, his face searching mine. I could feel his heart beating quickly against my chest, matching my own rapid heart rate, and I wanted to close the gap and press my lips against his. I closed my eyes and then I felt him freeze.

He sat up and put his finger to lips, "shh"

I heard the soft splash too, as he gently placed me on the warm sand. I swear the sand shook as I felt footsteps on the island.

"Hello? Anyone?" I looked up at Lachlan and his face paled. He reached for his 'skin' and held it close to him. He got up, leaving me in the sheltered sands, trying to check out who was here.

"Hello?" A high-pitched female voice rang out too. "Did you make it here?"

I followed, tensing as I noticed Lachlan was doing the same. We stood together watching the opening between the screens. We waited for them to find us.

"Sahara?" Another woman's voice called out. "It's Melody. If you're here, call out to us."

Lachlan lifted an eyebrow in question and looked at me. He took a step back and nodded. I nodded with acknowledgment, and knew I had to call out.

"Melody?" I called back, the shake in my voice betraying my confidence.

"Sahara, you made it!" Namiko peeked her head around the screen, Kai followed her around the screen but stopped short.

"What are you doing here, Selkie?" The disdain was dripping from his voice and Lachlan's facial hair bristled in alarm. *Selkie!* I thought. That's the mythological creature, that's right. But the way Kai said it made it sound like an insult.

"Saving the girl, mermaid." Lachlan fired back.

"As if anyone would want a *Selkie* to save them." Melody said icily.

Namiko came towards me quietly, not taking part in the verbal sparring. She looked me up and down.

"Are you alright?" She asked quietly. "Have you changed?"

"I'm fine. I think. Changed how? What's going on?" I asked aloud.

"See?" Kai sneered, "the stupid animal didn't even tell her what happened." Lachlan moved forward to protect me, but I stepped around him.

"Explain what exactly? I've been on the island for nearly two days now and no one has told me a goddamn fucking thing." I folded my arms on my chest and stood there. Melody laughed and walked towards me.

"Stupid human, Araxie is going to love your voice being added to her collection." She lifted a finger and reached for my throat. I slapped her hand away and she fell back laughing. "Selkie, darling. You should don your skin if you don't want us to take it from you." She reached for the hide held in his arms, sneering. He snatched it close and moved to throw it on. I watched as the man was swallowed by the skin and there was a very large seal where Lachlan had just stood. He was blue-grey and spotted, with long white whiskers from his cute black nose. I just stared, awestruck, as I watched the transformation again. Melody laughed and clapped. "That's a good boy. Now run along out to sea and bark at the seagulls." He turned his big puppy eyes at me, and I swear I could see the *'I'm sorry'* he was sending my way. When I nodded, he started waddling towards the beach.

Namiko moved beside me and took my arms and pulled me towards the water. "Since you're still alive on this island, you must have made a deal with the sea, right? " She asked me as we got closer to the waves washing ashore.

Melody was still laughing and kicking after Lachlan who was moving slowly on land.

"Deal with the sea?" I asked her.

"Oh, you must have hit your head. Hey Kai, we'll need to explain things to her before we bring her down." And then it dawned on me. They got to this island. There must be a way to get off the island, but something seemed twisted and wrong. My stomach knotted, and I didn't want their help. Why did they send Lachlan away?

"What the fuck is going on? How did you get here to find me?" I pulled my arms out of Namiko's grip.

"We swam. And we'll explain things to you. But please stay calm. We'll sit on the beach and show you, too."

Calm down? Fuck calming down! I wanted answers. Now. Like what happened?

Where was I? Why did they send Lachlan away? Why did he listen? It felt like when parents were talking in code about something grown up that I couldn't understand. But I could understand if anyone would fucking tell me! I was seething, but I knew that blowing up was going to get me hurt or possibly killed, judging by the sneers on their faces. So, I held in my rage and followed the three people who sent my saviour away to the beach.

Namiko plopped cross-legged onto the sand, back straight up and looked out at the sea. Melody waltzed up and laid herself lounge-style, propping her torso up by her elbows as relaxed as could be. Kai traipsed up and unceremoniously plopped down, legs splayed and straight out. I sat down in the sand, tucking my legs underneath me, wishing the sand would carry me away.

"So. Will someone please explain to me what is going on?" I asked.

"Ooh. Feisty. I like that" Kai winked at me. I'm pretty sure I visibly recoiled, with disgust apparent on my face.

"Hush, Kai. She's scared and has no idea what's going on." Namiko said quietly, shutting him up.

"Well, first things first. Congratulations on your transformation and welcome to the world of the sea." Melody announced with an air of regality.

"The Sea has chosen to make a deal with you. Instead of drowning, you have been given a second life," continued Kai. Namiko rolled her eyes and reached for my hand.

"What they are trying to say is: you are now a part of this world and not the human world anymore. And in this world, merfolk are the rulers." She looked at me, whether she expected me to say something or freak out, I didn't know. I just nodded, and gripped the sand tighter, as my hands balled into fists.

"You're a siren now." Melody stated with a sigh. "Which means, when you go into the water, you will grow scales on your body and your feet will turn into fins."

"You will be able to breathe underwater, but you won't be able to speak. Most sirens have adopted forms of sign language to talk with the rest of the merfolk." Namiko explained.

Kai looked at me. "Remember when I asked if you knew the difference between mermaids and sirens? Well, we," He gestured at the three of them lounging on the beach, "are mermaids. We were born of the sea. You," he pointed at me, "are a siren, transformed by the sea. You serve her, by serving us."

"A siren's voice can only be heard above the water." Namiko explained further. I sat in silence for a moment, processing what they were telling me, but it still seemed so farfetched.

"Alright, if I go into the water, I become a mute siren, but able to breathe underwater, so I won't drown?"

"Well, technically you have already drowned." Melody stated, sighing again and rolled onto her back to soak up the sun. "Oh, and we already told the police what happened on the island. You slipped while leaning too far over to hear your voice. Anyone who falls into Echo Cavern dies. No bodies are ever found. No one is searching for you." She rested her hands behind her red hair and closed her eyes.

What the fuck? I'm sure it flashed across my face. *They pushed me into the cavern to kill me, for what reason?*

"Look, your voice is the reason we did it. It's beautiful. I'm sure it's even more so since you've transformed." Namiko said, her eyes downcast. She at least looked a little remorseful and had a touch of sadness in her voice. Melody looked as though it was just another Tuesday.

"By the way," Kai asked, " how did you get tangled up with the Selkie?" I thought about it for a minute. I didn't trust these three. They just admitted to killing me, for my voice! They pushed me in and told everyone I slipped and died. Even if I did believe their story, something was wrong. I didn't make any deals with the sea. Even Lachlan had said he'd never met a siren like me. *Siren*, he had called me that, too! He took care of me and stood to protect me. These guys were talking about him like he was *beneath them*. *Merfolk rule*. They make the rules. But I wasn't like them.

"Uh, he was here on the island when I crawled up from the sea. I was so disoriented. He showed me the shelter, and where I could find food." I shrugged. I was going to have to act the part and figure out what was going on, who I could trust. Although, I didn't think I was going to have much choice in what they did next. I was at their mercy to get off this isolated island. I looked at Namiko, who at least sounded like she might help me, if the other two weren't there.

"So, I cannot drown?" She nodded. "That's good, but I'm still terrified of water. I don't know how to swim. Can I just stay here, and wait out this "deal" or whatever?" The three of them looked at me and just blinked.

"You can't SWIM?!" laughed Melody, clutching her stomach, nearly in tears.

"This will be fun!" Kai said, laughing along.

"One other thing that is very important for her to know," said Namiko.

"After" Kai and Melody said together. They both stood up and went to the water's edge.

"Watch what happens, Sahara. It's amazing." They waded into the water. Melody's legs came together, and her lower half turned a bright forest green. She dove under water, and I saw a flick of a green tail lift out of the water and follow her. I stared, transfixed. *Mermaids are real!*

Kai smiled, waved, and backflipped; a light cerulean blue tail followed behind him. Their heads peeked up over the water, hair slicked back.

"Nam, bring her into the water. Sahara, we will teach you how to swim with your legs together, and how to breathe. Small steps." Kai called back.

Namiko stood up and held her hand to me. She almost seemed reluctant, not looking directly at me.

"I'm afraid of water." I stated, not getting up.

"There is nothing in it that can hurt you. You are a siren, and thus you are the top of the ocean creatures." Namiko replied. When she put it that way, there really was no reason, other than fear, and Dad had always said "fear is no excuse." The exception was drowning. My mother had drowned so I feared drowning in water. But now I couldn't drown.

"Are all girls who drown turned into Sirens?" I asked suddenly.

"Most are given the choice to serve the Ocean. Some don't choose to serve, usually if they are taking their own lives. But most do." She answered.

My mother drowned. Would she have agreed to the choice? Would she have chosen a second life? For me? Could she be alive underwater? I might find her!

"OK. I can do this " I said aloud, trying to encourage myself. If I take the plunge, maybe I can overcome this fear.

Namiko waded in, and her lower torso turned a salmon pink colour. She was so pretty.

She held her hand out and helped me walk into the water.

This time I noticed my skin turning red and scales appeared. It didn't hurt, but it was a bright scarlet red.

I stopped and stared. Kai and Melody swam up.

"You can do it!" Kai encouraged, his blue tail swishing in the water beneath him, nearly disappearing into the blue water. His tail was pretty, too. His Hawaiian shirt had changed from a shirt to a tattoo of Hawaiian flowers on his torso that flowed into his cerulean blue tail. It was kind of amazing, as I stared at his transformation.

Melody had gone under water and hadn't resurfaced.

"Anything you want to ask?" Namiko said.

"Yes. If I do this, where are you going to take me?" I shuddered.

"A beautiful place I like to call home." She smiled and kept moving forward and sort of tugging me along. I was nearly up to my waist in the water and my legs were all red scales. I wasn't freaking out or upset. In fact, it was kind of interesting. Had I always been able to do this?

Namiko was smiling, but something seemed sad in her eyes. Kai was encouraging me to just dive in. I looked back at the island and thought to rush back, but

I didn't think going backwards was an option, living on that island would be a death sentence, especially if no one was looking for me. I was trapped and the only way out was forward.

I decided to go for it and took my last breath of fresh air.

I held my breath and put my face into the water. The cool water felt refreshing against my hot cheeks. I felt Namiko dive under and opened my eyes. There was a licking sound as something that felt like a lens popped into my eye. It was a yellow colour, which filtered out the natural blue. I could see under the water! I gasped, sucking in some water.

Kai's cerulean tail now appeared a much lighter blue and was distinct from the ocean. Namiko's tail was brighter than the salmon I thought it was. They swam past the dune and dove down toward some unseen barrier.

I ripped my face from the water and ran full speed to the island, stumbling through the sand.

I got out of the water and kept running, tripping over the palm trees and other debris.

The island was small, and I was in the middle of a coconut grove when I heard them shouting again.

Gotta hide! Gotta hide! I thought, looking for something, anything to hide me away from getting into the water.

"Find her!" The Irish accent echoed across the isle and I trembled.

"Drag her into the water if you must. Once she's transformed, she'll be stuck as a siren until her service is complete."

What? Permanently a siren? I shuddered and looked for something. The shelter and the screens were all that was there.

I was going to be caught. No question about it. I leaned against the palm tree and tried to calm my breathing, trying to keep them from finding me.

If I keep moving, maybe they'll think I ran and dove off the other side to escape them.

The more I thought about it, the more I realised the sea WAS my only escape. It's either water or water and if I face my fear, it's on my own terms.

I tried to calculate how far the beach was and stood up, full of resolve to get away from these murderous meatheads.

It's about forty feet to the water, then another twenty feet before the dunes run out, I estimated. I have no idea how to actually swim, but maybe if I transform like before I might know how.

I started to run, the sand a comforting feeling beneath my feet. I heard a shout!

"She's running for the beach!" Followed by the sound of pattering feet. They weren't as swift on the sand as I was, and I kept going, running full speed. It felt like the sands were carrying me and moving the obstacles out of my way. I just kept running.

I hit the beach as I saw Kai's body in my peripheral vision. *Shit.* I pushed my legs harder as I hit the water. The extra weight of the water slowed me down, and then there were warm arms around my waist lifting me out. I kicked and screamed "LET ME GO!" And to my shock he dropped me. I fell into the water on my ass and felt my legs start to glue together

No, no, no. I pushed myself up to try to stand but my legs weren't listening to me. I floundered for a bit trying to stand, to push away from Kai but then there was another set of arms around my chest, pulling me backwards. I fell back and screamed. I swung my arms and they collided with something hard. I heard an "oof" and the arms behind me fell away, but then grabbed my right arm. Another pair of hands grabbed my left arm. The two mermaids were pulling me, dragging me to the deeper water. I struggled with the two, trying to kick my now solidified legs and scarlet fins as Kai came close. I reached over and bit the hand on my right side. Melody yelped in pain but did not let go, and Kai came closer.

The girls held my arms steady, and he pushed my head under water.

"Let me go!" I screamed but the water filled my throat and I sputtered. I lifted my head up, but the yellow filter in my eyes had settled, and my neck had that funny feeling of water rushing in.

"Why the hell did you let her go?" Melody asked Kai.

"Why did you?!" He yelled back.

"It doesn't matter," Namiko said quietly. "She transformed fully; she can't return now. " I looked down and realised she was right. Then, a stinging feeling numbed my right cheek as Melody slapped me!

"Serves you right, bitch." Melody snorted, then grabbed my hair.

"Ow. Let me go, you stupid bitch!" I shouted, swinging my arm at her.

She let go and I fell into the water face first.

"Good, now she's mute. Let's get her down to the city. Ashera is going to love this one." Kai said.

Namiko just shook her head, her eyes looked sad, but she nodded.

"Come on Sahara, we will take you to Aquacity, where all the merfolk live. There will be more sirens there."

I opened my mouth to shout no, but Melody slapped me again. I stared at her, ready to swing back.

"Remember, you're mute. You can't make noise unless your head is above water. I suggest you don't bother wasting your energy and instead learn how to breathe and swim, you useless waste of a voice."

The stinging hurt my face, but the water was soothing. I closed my mouth and focused on breathing, letting the water in through my gills, and feeling the oxygen enter my body.

Just survive this. I thought as I let my body adjust to the new sensation. My mouth stayed firmly shut since I instinctively wanted to hold my breath. I concentrated on swishing my tail, *My tail!* and making the water move around me. My arms had turned a scarlet red, the scales shimmering in the sunlight that was filtered from above. I felt my head and face, and they too had grown scaly, with raised ridges on my face and even a few bumps of horn from my temples.

I looked at the mermaids flipping around and swimming circles around me. They were circling, waiting for me to do something.

"Have you ever seen a siren so ... bright?" Namiko asked, speaking to Kai and Melody.

"No, not like that. It's a little weird. Sirens are usually muted in greys, blues and browns." Kai answered.

It hit me then. Their tails were bright and scaled, but their upper torso remained human-like with skin and flesh and features. Mine had turned more creature-like.

"Who cares what colour she is. Probably a weird gene or something." Melody scoffed.

"Let's get her down to the dumping grounds for her initiation" she started to swim down.

"Come on, Sahara, flick your legs like this." Namiko swished her tail left then right, but her fin opposite that to propel herself forward.

I opened my mouth to ask how, but when the water came rushing down my throat, I quickly closed it again. *Yuck. Mute.*

I raised my arms and signed. "How do I turn?"

Namiko raised her eyes in surprise but showed me. She explained her movements, as I followed and managed to turn in a circle.

"Great," Namiko said. Now try to follow all my movements. By the time we get down to the meeting point, you should have the basics of swimming down.

I nodded my head as she moved in front of me, her pink tail flicking and swishing. I tried to copy her movements, but I was clumsy and not as graceful as she was. I could hear Kai chuckling behind me, as I oversteered my tail and went careening out to the side. Melody had grown impatient and swam ahead, leaving me with Kai and Namiko.

He didn't say much, and his mouth was drawn in a thin line, concentrating on something he wasn't thrilled about. Namiko didn't seem like she wanted to be doing this at all. *So, what's forcing them?* I thought.

"Hey Nam, the north or west entrance?" He called out to her, coming out of his deep thoughts.

"I'm thinking the east. With her bright colour and poor swimming skills, we should keep her out of the major channels and currents until she has time to learn with the other sirens."

We had been descending quite a bit and I was concentrating on my tail movements and breathing when I accidentally swam into a stopped Namiko. She smiled and pointed out to the water in front of me.

Rising from the dark blue was a large dome, with buildings made of coral and rock in the center. At the top of the dome there seemed to be an oval arena, or colosseum and there was an obvious trapped air pocket at the top.

Kai pointed to it, saying "that's where the sirens practice their song. It's also where we will be passing you off to Ashera."

I signed to Namiko, "What are the other buildings?"

"Those other buildings are our homes, schools, restaurants, businesses, the usual things you find in a city. Outside of Aquacity there are seaweed farms, fish farms and other agriculture-like things. " Namiko explained.

"But we've got to get you to the east gate, and straight up the dome to the air pocket."

"They're holding auditions later today, and you'll definitely want to pass." Kai said and started to swim around to the east side.

"Auditions?" I signed to Namiko. *"What am I auditioning for?"*

"For a place in the Royal Siren Choir" she said, "and for your life" she mumbled as she flicked her tail. She swam upwards a bit and then swerved to the left. I followed, my skin chilled, but my unnatural and ungraceful ass was flailing again as I careened out of control.

As I got closer, I noticed the flurry of activity - er, well, the bubbles of activity in the city. There seemed to be buildings both carved into the rock and grown out of coral. The dome itself was translucent and made from some sort of semi-permeable material.

The two mermaids swam up to the east side and then towards an opening about halfway down the dome. Kai passed through the gate first.

"This is going to sting," Namiko said as she grabbed my hand and pulled me through the membrane.

It felt like I'd been shocked and stabbed with thousands of little needles as I was pulled through. I opened my mouth to scream and just swallowed water. I started to cough and sputter.

Kai smacked me on the back.

"Attagirl. Didn't even pass out!" He looked genuinely pleased.

What the hell was that? I signed.

"Jellyfish membrane. Keeps out unwanted mammals and other little nasties."

"Most first timers aren't usually awake after that! How are you feeling?" He asked and a look of concern crossed his features.

"The jellyfish will stop stinging in a couple moments. Then we'll follow that channel to the top of the fishbowl." He pointed at a current of water that seemed to be flowing a bit differently from the water we were in. It reminded me of transportation tubes like the ones in sci-fi movies, except they were tubes of fast running water.

"Once you're in the channel, just let it carry you." Namiko said, pointing.

Watching Kai swim up to it, he checked the column of water and then dove in. The current inside picked him up and sent him toward the air pocket at the top.

"Don't worry! It's not as dramatic as Kai. Just swim into it and relax. I will be with you." She held her hand out.

Why am I being forced into this? I signed to her. She had seemed to be reluctant and almost remorseful this whole time. Now that Kai was gone and Melody had ditched us, maybe I could get an answer.

I'm being forced as much as you. She signed, after glancing and checking for someone. *I can't explain it. But I must do it. I'm so sorry.*

"Come on, Sahara, into the channel." Her tone was firm, but her eyes were soft, and I realised she told the truth. She was being forced into this, too. What could they have on her to coerce her into drowning someone and pressuring them into becoming a siren?

She pulled my arm towards the current. I opened my mouth and said, "I'm sorry." The words echoed under the water and rang clear through the area.

Namiko's eyes widened in shock, and she clamped a hand over my mouth and shoved me into the channel.

The sound of rushing water filled my ears, and I couldn't hear or think. I tried to follow Namiko's advice and just relax, but it was proving difficult. It felt a little like an elevator and the roaring sounds of open car windows on the highway, combined into a loud roar.

I closed my eyes and braced for impact when strong hands grabbed me and pulled me out of the rushing water. I seemed to float where I was left, trying to regain my balance, but my head just kept spinning.

"Oh sure, the channel is what broke her." Kai's voice rang out. I opened my eyes and stared into his brown eyes. The ponytail had fallen out and his dark curly hair was loose in the water, billowing out. The tattoos on his torso looked like they were pulsing with the refracted light. I reached out to steady myself on his chest, when Namiko pulled me toward her.

"Don't make a sound." She whispered urgently in my ear. She turned herself to have her back to Kai. She looked me in the eye and took my hand and started finger spelling on my hand, so Kai could not see.

You. Can. Not. Speak. You. Will. Be. Killed. The urgency in her eyes and the force of the letters on my hand made me wince.

I swallowed the water in my mouth, getting used to the sensation of constantly having fluids. I nodded.

What the fuck. Are Sirens not mute? Was I different somehow?

Namiko tugged my arm and pulled me close, "nod if you understood." I nodded. And then she smiled and turned to Kai.

"Ready to bring her to meet Ashera?" She asked Kai.

"About as ready as I'll ever be. That woman's voice is enough to make me go crazy!"

"Alright, let's go."

Kai swam toward an opening at the bottom of the dome. The colosseum-like structure was constructed of stone and granite, with statues of merfolk carvings. The opening was covered with hanging seaweed, like door beads.

I hesitated before swimming through the opening, prompting Kai to giggle.

"Only the dome has jellyfish-covered openings. And that was a mild one. The nasty ones are in the jails and holding cells."

Jails. Holding cells. Are you freaking kidding me? I swam through and entered a tunnel. I couldn't see at first, but then a sort of glow emanated from my eyes and I could make out shapes. I swam into the walls a few times, the tunnel too narrow for my amateurish swimming techniques.

Then the tunnel opened up into a huge arena. There were seats and a bowl, and the air was just up there. I tried to swim for it, but then suddenly there were two hands on my arms.

"Why are you here?" The person to my left asked. I looked at him. His tail was a golden-yellow colour and he was wearing a set of gold cuffs around his wrists. He carried a spear in his left hand and held me with his right. His chest was bare, but he had a helmet on his head.

"Afternoon, Captain. We're bringing Ashera a new recruit to audition for the Royal Siren Choir, Sir."

"She's a new siren?" He asked, his voice laced with scepticism. "She's too bright."

"See, I told you her colour was weird." Kai said to Namiko, "But we watched her transform this morning and have just brought her in."

"Very well. Take her below. Ashera is prepping the remaining new recruits before we lower the water level."

"Yes sir!" The hands released me, and I was shoved into Kai's torso.

He wrapped his arms around me and whispered in my ear. "Still feisty, aren't you?"

I pushed away from his chest and tried to slap him, but the momentum from pushing myself back carried and I just tumbled over, and over. The two guards laughed as I just kept spinning.

"Definitely new."

"This show will be entertaining today. I might make my way up to see."

Kai finally grabbed my arm and pulled me in, stabilizing me. Namiko led the way, and Kai held onto my hand and led me into another tunnel. We swam lower and lower, reaching sand on the bottom. I heard a voice calling out.

"Come on, ladies, swim up and draw your number for your audition." The voice was not as feminine as Namiko's, but not masculine.

Kai pulled me along as I reached down to touch the sand. Beautiful sand, it felt like a caress. I missed my desert and felt the urge to cry.

Rounding the corner there were about a dozen creatures behind a jellyfished opening. They all turned to look at me, with their glowing yellow eyes. They had legs, with fins at the end that were swishing around, like the merfolk, but their entire bodies were covered in scales, in varying shades of blue, green, browns and mute oranges. There were ridges and dimples formed on their chests, arms and faces and several had horns on their heads.

"Ashera, we've got a new one." Kai called. A couple of the creatures flinched back, and a mermaid turned around.

"She's red," she stated flatly before turning back to the creatures. "Come on, ladies, get your numbers, or I'll brand you with them."

What the hell? I thought. *Ladies? And was this a holding cell? Why are they behind jellyfish?* And it hit me. *Sirens.* Those creatures were sirens. I reached for my face and felt the dimples and ridges and realised I looked like they did. They weren't creatures. I was. Kai then pushed me towards Ashera.

"Follow her instructions and you won't die."

Namiko signed a quick *sorry* before swimming off. I was left alone with Ashera and the rest of the Sirens.

"Choose your number" she said and held a bucket out. It was filled with pearls. I reached in and grabbed one.

"Congrats, Red, you're number eleven out of twelve. Hope they don't like the first five or there will be no spots left." She pointed to an alcove with a bench carved into the wall. "Wait there, and we'll get the stadium set for your auditions." Then she swam away into a little tunnel and was gone.

E leven pairs of eyes were trained on me, silently staring. I stared back. They were not pretty creatures, they were dark, angry, and vicious looking. A siren with dull greyish blue scales swam towards the jellyfish covered door. Her yellow eyes looked at me, but there was sympathy in them. She signed, *"you alright?"*. I could see the other sirens look at her with interest, and then back at me. I nodded back to her. She smiled, and I saw the sharp pointed teeth that adorned her mouth. I recoiled and brought my hand to my mouth. I ran my tongue over my own teeth and found that my teeth were still my own. They weren't filed into sharp points, and I didn't have fangs. I relaxed a little as I looked back at the sirens.

"*My name is S-A-H-A-R-A. You?*" I signed to them. They looked at me in surprise, whether it's because I gave them my name, or because I already knew how to sign, I didn't know.

The grey-blue Siren signed back "*M-A-Y-A.*"

"Alright Ladies, time to get some air and hear those darling voices." Ashera sang as she swished her bright yellow tail through the passageway. "Line up in your number order and follow me." She grabbed a stick and pulled the jellyfish curtain back, allowing the Sirens out. There were looks of pure hatred crossing their features as they moved out and got into line. A couple signed a quick "Hello" with their name to me as they passed.

"*P-A-S-H-A,*" signed a dull bluish-teal siren.

"*R-A-I-D-N-E,*" signed a tannish-brown siren, with some intricate curling horns coming from her head.

"*N-I-X-I-E,*" signed an earthy green siren, whose colour resembled moss growing on an old tree.

They were sirens four, five and seven. I got in line as number eleven and Maya followed behind me as twelve.

We swam through the little tunnels, and I bumped into Maya several times and held us up. The tenth siren just shook her head and blew bubbles in frustration.

"You're brand new?" Maya signed, asking me. I nodded to her,

"I never swam before today." Her yellow eyes flashed, and widened, but a smile crept across her face. She held out her hand for me to take and she helped me swim the tunnels. I only bumped into the walls a couple more times, then there was light coming from the end of the tunnel and I could see the walls.

We entered a wide-open arena. The water level had dropped since I had been through the seats with Kai and Namiko. I looked around and saw that some of the seats were occupied, some above water, and some below. Mermaids and squids, octopus and dolphins, and even a shark or two were occupying seats under the water. Above the water level, were tortoises, seals, and a pair of otters holding hands. There appeared to be humans too, but looking closely, they were probably shape shifters. "Alright ladies, first audition begins in five minutes. You may surface, and one of you teach Red the siren song." Ashera sing-songed before closing the gate with another jellyfish curtain. We were trapped in the arena.

The other sirens swam upwards, to the open air. Maya pulled me with her, and as we surfaced, the girl's heads transformed into human heads. They were all beautiful.

There was a collective gasp of air as they took in their first breaths. I followed along, and since they were all quiet, I remained quiet, too. Maya and Pasha pulled me aside. They spoke to me in hushed whispers, never letting a note really ring from their voices. It sounded very guttural from their throats.

"I'm sorry this happened to you." said Maya.

"What's-" Pasha clamped a hand over my mouth. "Shh" She whispered.

"You can't use your siren voice. Only throat sounds." She looked around and pointed at the guards above the water line, and I noticed the harpoons that were trained on each of us. My eyes opened in shock as I realised I was in serious danger.

"If you ring out a sound other than when you sing, they will shoot you in the throat. This makes you in-capable of completing the deal with the sea, and after your time, you just turn into foam instead." I nodded and lifted my hands.

"I can sign, my dad was deaf."

"Signing is great, but the merfolk can read what we say." Pasha said. She had long straight black hair, and beautiful brown eyes. Her skin tone had settled into a pretty, dark caramel colour. I raised my arms and noticed they had changed to my usual colour. Maya was a natural olive colour, which still complemented her tail colours.

"Okay. what do I do?" I followed it by gesturing around the arena.

"We sing the siren's call song. If we can make the shift above the water and dive into the sea, we get to live. But only five will be selected for the Siren's choir." Maya explained, her throaty voice grating on my nerves.

"Listen to the other sirens when they sing. We all must sing the same song." "Were you drowned naturally, or did the mermaids drown you?" asked Maya suddenly.

I held up two fingers to choose the second one.

"Ok good, you already had a good voice, and can probably sing. This will be a bit easier."

"AQUACITY CITIZENS, VOLUNTEERS AND JUDGES, PLEASE TAKE YOUR POSTS ABOVE AND BELOW THE WATER. The auditions are about to commence." A voice rang out throughout the water. I could not see where it was.

I saw a pair of seals swim to a place half above and below. The one on the left reminded me of Lachlan, and I had to blink twice. The seal beside him was grey and white, and smaller. It gave off a feminine vibe, and I was sure they were a pair of Selkies.

Ashera swam up and called out. "Ladies, only one of you may sing at a time. You must get the volunteers to jump into the sea with your call. You cannot chat or make other calls or songs. You may listen to the other ladies. First up, swim to the centre and begin." A young woman with a short, blond pixie cut swam to the centre.

She stopped and took a deep breath. Then she let out a piercing scream. My ears rang in pain, as she kept screaming. There was a small thud, and her scream was cut short. A harpoon stuck out of her throat, and she sank under the water. Ashera shook her head. "Always at least one. Glad that we got that out of the way ... LADIES, you will sing, or you will be left to rot."

She pulled the harpoon from the struck Siren, and then pushed her down. Two Guards with the gold helmets grabbed her arms and took her through a different jellyfish door than the one we came through. I was shocked, and just watched the madness. Will I survive this?

"Just sing the song. It's better to sing and get some freedoms in the city, than to be left in a cell with no purpose." Maya whispered, a tear falling down her face.

"Number two, begin your song." Another woman swam up and took a breath. I braced my ears for the screeching but was pleasantly surprised to find her voice was beautiful. The song was haunting and melodic. There were no words, just sounds that almost sounded like words sung. It was familiar, but new and incredible. I heard a splash as someone jumped into the water and turned my head to where I heard it. A merman had jumped into the arena. He stayed underwater.

A couple more splashes were heard as she finished her song. "Good, number two. You pass, please proceed to the left of the arena. She swam quietly over there, but a somber expression was on her face.

"Number three, please proceed to the center." Ashera's voice called out. A few more from the seats had gone above the water, and the three that had jumped in returned to their seats.

The next girl sang the same song, but she faltered a little, and no one jumped into the arena. Two guards swam up and carried her down to the same jellyfish door as the first number. Number four was Pasha. She swam out and sang the same song beautifully. Three quick splashes later and she had passed the test. She swam to the left of the arena with number two.

Raidne swam out next, and her voice was crystal and echoing, and she also got her required volunteers into the water. Number six sang the whole song, but her key was off and only one jumped. She was led down to the jellyfished door.

"What happens to them?" I signed to Maya. She just shrugged, her eyes watching them pass through the door. She was twirling her hair around her fingers, showing signs of nervousness.

Nixie was up next, and she nailed it. What I wouldn't give for these women's voices in my choir. Then I remembered that I was technically dead and life didn't matter anymore.

Numbers eight, nine and ten all failed, and were led away through the door. I started to get nervous. But I also knew I could nail that song.

"Number Eleven. Ah, our newest siren, Red." I shook my head. I had the song memorized now, and it was a minor, my favourite to sing.

I opened my mouth and let out the musical notes. My voice echoed in the space, ethereal, haunting, and beautiful. I used my full range, held the notes, and waited for the splashes.

I heard three, then four, then another few. I ended the song and looked around. All of the creatures were staring at me from the water. The volunteers had jumped. The otters, the seals and tortoises had all jumped in. The guards bearing the harpoons had abandoned them and dove in too.

Ashera looked shaken, and it took a moment for anyone to react.

"Number eleven passed." her voice was shaking. She swam to the guards to discuss something with them. They all got out of the water in states of dazzlement and confusion. I swam to the other girls on the left side of the arena.

I heard a whisper from Pasha, "what the hell was that?" When I turned her eyes were full of worry and confusion. "I wanted to drown in your voice! Sirens don't affect other sirens."

Nixie whispered "The guards are wearing hearing protection. They shouldn't have even been affected!"

I was confused. Had I done something wrong? I sat and listened to Maya sing, and the three volunteers all jumped in. She joined us on the left side but gave me a wide berth while the other girls congratulated her. There were six of us remaining on the left side and six who had failed.

Then Ashera swam up to us.

"Well done, ladies. Six of you have passed, but there are only five spots in the choir, so we will still have to cut one of you from our ranks. We will have you sing together and whoever fails to harmonize with me will be cut." I looked around and blanched. I was too new; I didn't know their songs. Just this one.

The others looked just as confused and terrified.

"We only know the one song" one whispered to another.

"Alright, ladies. Swim to the centre. Our judges will be the two selkie ambassadors, Lachlan and Aerwyna, and our resident dolphin ambassador, Philip. The three of them jumped into the water and held their heads up.

"Great. The animals are judging. Like they can understand." I heard a whisper from the one who didn't give me her name.

"The merfolk understand them." Nixie whispered back.

I just gazed silently, watching Lachlan. I was drawn to watch him swim. He was so graceful for such a large animal. The girl ... Ar something. She was circling around him, and I felt a flash of anger. He caught me watching him, and I turned to look away. I'm sure my cheeks reddened. I tried to focus on the dolphin, but he was blowing bubbles, and I struggled not to laugh out loud.

Ashera called out to the judges "Are you ready?"

I heard three distinct yeses from the animals and held my head up high.

Ashera looked at us and said, "harmonize with me. The judges will choose the one who is out of harmony." And she began to sing a tune I didn't know.

T he tune was simple, almost like a lullaby. Ashera's voice was beautiful, but a touch flat.

The song was full of long notes, repeated again. Once she had repeated it a second time, Nixie and Raidne joined in.

They complimented her notes in thirds, one pitching higher and the other lower, and the tune became deeper, fuller and more rounded. That was what she and the judges wanted.

After two repeats, number two and Pasha joined, again harmonizing in thirds.

The song was beautiful, almost a perfect balance of pitch and tone. I heard a wobble, from number two but she corrected it.

The next round was mine and Maya's turn to join, and I thought about the song, and how it could be improved. Maya chose to go lower thirds with her harmonics, but this song could be totally full with a fifth higher. I went for it, levelling my notes with the full fifth harmonized. The audience stopped talking to one another as the seven of us sang in harmony. We sang for four more rounds. I held my notes as long as Ashera and closed out the end of the round on a minor. The resonance in the arena was replaced by the echoing silence that fell over everyone.

No one moved for what felt like a lifetime. Then I heard a clap. One of the guards was clapping from his perch. The other guards joined in, and then the turtles were flapping, the jellyfish bobbed up and down rapidly, the merfolk watching and clapping as well.

"I've never heard anything quite like that."

"Beautiful sound."

"Ashera will have to train them to make that new sound."

"How haunting."

"I would happily die listening to their voices."

"I think our choir just got six new additions instead of five."

The comments kept flowing, hurtling past my ears. I heard them, but I was also on edge. I hadn't mimicked the rest of them. I hadn't gone in the traditional thirds that the rest did. I took it up to a fifth and let the notes ring, my single high note balanced with the notes below. It was a beautiful song. When I looked at the other sirens, they were staring at me, mouths open in shock.

Well. Maybe I will be taken to prison. I thought. *Or wherever they took the other sirens who didn't pass.*

"Ashera," Philip the dolphin said. "That red siren is different."

"Trouble." Ashera replied. Then she signalled to the guards.

"No, I don't mean in a 'she's going to change the pH level.' I mean, she's something different from what other girls are. She's brighter, her voice is stronger, balanced with a roundness that the others don't have. Not even the merfolk have that tone to it." He continued as Ashera's face twisted.

"She's certainly unique. Pretty, too. Her vocal abilities exceed the other girls, and her voice held even the merfolk captive. But I agree with Phil, there's something about the girl that just screams 'look at me'". The girl seal said. I turned my head to listen when I heard Lachlan speak.

"It would be best to introduce her to the Choir and get her under supervision. The folks around here are going to notice her. Also, if you still need to cut, it's number two." Lachlan said, not even glancing at me. I tried to swim toward the other girls who were staring at Ashera and the judges.

I tried my throat whisper. "At least they are saying nice things?" I said to Maya.

"What do you mean?" She responded. "The judges only have good things to say."

"You can understand them?" Her eyes flicked back and forth.

"You can't?" I signed back, noticing that Ashera was swimming back.

"Only those born of the sea can talk with the sea creatures and shifters." She replied.

Oh. I thought. What the hell was I? I'm a siren, that much has been established. Lachlan was sure of that too. But I was a brighter colour. My dark red tail flashed below me, and my white dress still billowed beneath me. I was quite sure I had transformed the first time I was under water. I don't remember making a deal with the sea. She didn't talk to me. I didn't pray or even have time to ask for more life, and to be totally honest, I don't think I drowned.

Out of the corner of my eye I saw the guards move in, and then two were bringing the number two siren into the other tunnel. The guards and Ashera led the way silently under the water. I waved to the judges as I lowered myself into the water fully again.

I was going to miss my air, but Maya grabbed my hand and pulled me down with her. We followed them through many dark corridors. I was getting used to my glowing eyes when we arrived at a hallway filled with doors. There were no jellyfish, just seaweed barriers over the arching doorways on the sides.

Ashera then began her explanation.

"Welcome to your new home. Each of you has a room here. There is a common area at the end of the hall. Once you meet the rest of the choir, you will complete the assignments given to you by the Queen and the Sea. With successful missions, you will earn privileges within the city. For now, you are confined to this hallway. There are two guards posted, and they will accompany you to most places for a while. The remaining choir should be back from their latest mission at around midnight. There is a pocket of air in the common area so you may speak freely, but absolutely NO SINGING. if we catch any song, you will lose your throat, and then be cast out of Aquacity."

I looked around and tried to come to terms with my new surroundings.

Another trapped situation. How did I keep getting into these? Ashera pointed straight down the hall. I followed Maya and Pasha into the common area. There were benches and a table with a counter. Another box made from woven material floated above my head. The air pocket. I swam up and took a breath, savouring the oxygen.

The other girls did the same. The baskets had some simple fruits in them. I hungrily bit into a pear. *Can I wake up from this horrible nightmare yet?*

The five of us sat in silence in the air pocket, each lost in her own thoughts.

I heard the crunch of an apple and chewing to my left.

Pasha, the siren with bluish, teal-coloured scales was staring blankly ahead, her big round eyes were glazed over. She was chewing robotically. Her dark hair had dried some from sitting in the air and was frizzing up around her face. It was sticking up, almost as if she had been electrocuted.

Raidne, the earthy-toned brown and green scaled siren, had limp, dirty blond hair and was leaning against the wall. Her olive skin took on a green hue in the limited light of the alcove. The alcove itself was like a cavern with an up-sloped floor. We were definitely still under the colosseum. There was stone furniture, if you could call it that, shaped into a table that sat above the water line. There were stone benches below the line. There were recesses in the walls above the water line that appeared to have various dishes and cutlery, but the only food seemed to be the fruit in the basket that floated by.

Another crunch of her apple from Pasha drew my eyes back to the lot of us sitting silently around the table. Maya was sitting with her face buried in her hands. She appeared to be almost napping, but her breathing kept changing. Her scales were a dull grey-blue, which really did not blend well with her human features. She had wide dark eyes and full lips. Her hair had fallen over her head in long, dark brown waves.

Nixie was playing with her fingers, using one of her green-blue scales to scrape underneath the nails. Her hair was straight, black and chin-length. Her human skin was very pale, and her features were of an Asian descent. She was pretty. They all were very beautiful. I guess I understood why the sailors told their siren stories. I looked at my own scales, a deep scarlet colour. Very bright compared to the other four in the room. My hair was a dark auburn, still double-braided from what I could tell. I longed for a mirror to see what the hell I looked like underwater.

My dress had started to fray along the hem, and I noticed the other women weren't wearing any clothing. I have no idea how I hadn't noticed before. None of the mermaids were wearing clothes either.

How had I not noticed a lack of covering? Were there breasts in my view this entire time and I just hadn't noticed?

No, that's not possible. Kai wore his shirt that magically became a tattoo on his torso. Did the girls have similar tattoos or markings? I looked at the girls in turn,

Pasha seemed to have a thin scarf that appeared over her breasts. It was like she was always wearing it, but it did not appear underwater.

Raidne seemed to have on a muted top, but it blended with her olive skin so well that she appeared to be very much the same above and below the water.

I couldn't tell with Maya since her chest was firmly planted on the stone table and her breathing was quite steady and shallow now.

Nixie had nude bathing suit material there, but they mostly appeared to be topless.

Now I was curious if my own body gave me modesty, or if it was something I had to conjure. Could I do that? Am I magical?

There was some commotion at the end of the hall and Maya stirred from the table. Her face now had the imprint of her hand and she looked sleepy.

"What is happening?" She signed.

The other three just shrugged. I looked down the hallway to where the guards were posted. There were a group of other sirens swimming in, and one siren was a bright royal blue. The rest were muted colours and they silently swam into the alcoves. They looked like they each had a room. The bright siren was blond, with two small horns in the same royal blue that was threaded atop her head. It looked almost like a crown. She swam down the hallway and into our common room. She looked at us and smiled. Her teeth were sharpened razors, and they looked especially elongated. Her nose was sunken and appeared to be barely raised. Her yellow eyes glowed brightly in the dim water. She lifted herself to sit on the bench beside Raidne, When she rose out of the water, her features softened, her eyes settled into a bright blue instead of yellow, and her teeth retracted. I watched as the gills on the side of her neck gave way to pristine porcelain skin so white it almost glowed. The triangle marking on her chest gave way to a blue halter top that tied around her neck. She sighed and looked at us in turn. She took a breath and spoke with a guttural sound that sounded like a fifty-year old woman who had smoked all her life.

"Welcome, sirens. We cannot speak below water. Do any of you know sign language?" She signed at the same time, and the five of us nodded yes.

"Great! I will continue to sign then. My name is Cordelia." She pointed at each of us in turn and learned our names.

"All of your names are water or sea-based names, except for yours," She pointed at me.

"Welcome to the siren's choir. I will give you a room to sleep tonight, and tomorrow we will go to the surface for a mission from the sea." she continued. "Once we are above the water, and on the beach of an island, we can talk a little more fully. Please follow me." She swam down the hallway and pointed us each to a room.

I was the last one given a room and she followed me into the space.

"You are a very brightly coloured siren." She signed. "Has anyone given you any trouble?"

I shook my head no, "I've only been a siren for a day. I can't even swim very well." She nodded and her sharp teeth peeked out from under a hard smile.

"We will talk more tomorrow once we get a chance to show you the deal you have made. Try and get some rest. Have a good night." She disappeared between the seaweed curtains, and I got a good look around my room. It was basically a small cell. There was a circle covered in moss that appeared to be the bed. There was no light, but my eyes were glowing enough to see the small space. I had grown a little more comfortable breathing the salty water, but I was sure I would be unable to sleep.

I curled up on the moss, and the scent was surprising. It smelled like oxygen, air and grass. I felt like I was on land. I was stroking my tail, feeling the thin membrane and marvelling at how I could both feel the sensation in my red hands and in my tail. I remember feeling afraid to fall asleep, and then nothing.

I was drowning, but I was on a beach, my legs were dry on the land, and I was standing, spitting, and coughing out water. I tried to run but fell face-first into the sand. The sand flowed down my throat, filing my lungs, and I tried to spit it up. The sand surrounded me, and I was sinking into it, I flailed my arms, and propelled myself through the sand. My legs glued themselves together, and I started kicking, propelling myself further into the sand. My lungs cried out in agony, needing air, and I finally gasped as I inhaled a mouthful of sand. But the sand wasn't hurting. In fact, I could breathe. I tried to stop flailing, and my eyes were glowing red. I could see in the sand, as if it was water. There were shadows ahead, some crabs, and conches and other debris buried in the sand. This wasn't right. I was underneath the sand, and I could feel each grain of sand against my body. The expected friction just bounced off my red skin. My scales had shifted to a metallic hardness. I could feel that the membrane at the base of my tail was rigid and something had grown out of my back. There was a hornlike appendage across my head, and I raised my hands to feel it. It was similar to the one on the blue Siren, intertwined like a crown. I kicked the sand to rise to the surface, and when I hit the air, I choked. I coughed and sputtered and let out a scream.

The movement in the hallway was quick and fast. I woke up with a group of sirens around me, and Cordelia's hand over my mouth. Her yellow eyes were in shock and wonder. Nervous energy filled the room.

She signed to the group "tell the guards we need a trip to the surface. NOW." I looked in surprise and awe at the group around me. Two sirens swam away, and Cordelia was pulling me along the corridor in their direction. The rest of the sirens grabbed all the other girls, and we filed silently into the hallway. The guards looked a bit taken aback but allowed Cordelia to take us out. We followed her through the twisting hallways and out of the colosseum and into the city.

She led us down the channel and over to the east gate. I flinched when I saw the jellyfish door frame again, but she just swam through, tugging me along with her.

The stinging was just as painful as before, and I nearly cried out again. She pulled me along, swimming south around the city dome, and then she raced to the surface. There was an island a little way south, and she pointed there. The sun had not yet risen, but we could see that the island was mostly underwater, with some rocks to sit on above water.

We all reached it and surfaced, our faces changing when we neared the surface. I wondered how and when it knew to change from siren to human, but then there were about ten of us, sitting around the rocks.

Cordelia screamed, it was so loud and awful sounding I felt like my own ears would start bleeding. I covered my ears with my hands and shrank down, trying to stop the sound from hurting.

She suddenly stopped and cleared her throat.

"Apologies, ladies," came a sign song in her beautiful, melodic voice. "The scream sends away any listening ears or eyes. It makes it so that we can speak above water, without bringing anyone to their deaths." She looked around the island, at the girls sitting there.

"It seems we have a new group who have joined the choir. First things first - I'm very sorry that you have entered into the agreement with the ocean. But I am happy to welcome you."

Pasha piped up "You mean you're sorry we were drowned?"

"Yes. I am sorry that you drowned at sea. But I am happy that the ocean gave you the option to commit to a second life once you have completed your service. Please tell me, how many years of service did she ask of you?" She pointed at Pasha.

"Seventy-five years." she said. Her voice was a deep alto concerto. Very different from the soprano I thought she had. Cordelia pointed at Raidne

'I have fifty years left." Raidne said, a true mezzo-soprano. "Ah, were the mermaids kind to you?" Cordelia asked.

"They only just discovered me about three months ago. They spent a lot of time teaching me sign language and explaining Aquacity and its rules. Had I not made the choir, I would have gone back to being solo in the sea." I thought it was strange that these girls knew their years of service and had even made a deal with the sea. What was this all about?

"I have a hundred years" Maya said, followed by Nixie saying "I have ninety eight to go."

"Such long services to provide" Cordelia said. "That's okay, we can work with that. There are a few of the older sirens who are finishing up in the next two years." She then looked at me, and asked "What about you, how many years did the sea ask from you?" "I -- I don't know." I looked down.

"How do you not know? Did you not make a deal with the sea?" Pasha asked me.

"I don't remember." Cordelia stared at me with a strange look in her eyes. I got the weird feeling that I shouldn't share my transformation story.

"I was pushed off a cliff, and then I just woke up in the water being led by mermaids. Oh my, that was yesterday morning." I left out details, and I got the sense that Cordelia was sizing up my story.

"I imagine that you haven't been to Donut Isle. Has anyone explained anything to you?" She asked nicely.

"Not really. I feel kind of trapped by the whole thing, considering I don't remember making a choice."

Cordelia sat back, and the older sirens bounded off the island swimming away for who knows what. That left the six of us.

Cordelia explained the basics of transformation; and the place we were living. We were in Aquacity, under the rule of the mermaids. Mermaids were able to change from sea to land after their twentieth birthday. Meaning, they could go on land anytime. Sirens were locked into their tails from the time they first transformed until their service was completed.

"What kind of services do we provide for the sea?" Nixie asked.

"Well, that depends on what she asks. Usually, we get a calling to sing to a passing ship. The sailors who jump are then drowned and their souls are given to the sea." "Wait, we murder people?" I asked suddenly. I felt sick. I wasn't going to send sailors to their death. My dad nearly died, and my mother … well, she did drown. I couldn't inflict that on anyone.

"Yes, the siren's songs we sing are to have a sailor jump off his ship or steer their ships into rocks. With our song in their ears, they do not suffer." "Are there any male sirens?" came Maya's question.

"No, and sirens cannot mate until after their service is complete. Once your service is complete, you can go on land and begin life anew."

"Well, damn. Can a siren mate with a merman?" she asked again,

"Do you fancy a merman, dear Maya?" Maya blushed and put her head down. "Sirens are made by the sea, and merfolk are born in it. When your service is done, you will be returned to your human form, at the age you appear now. If a merman is still interested in you, you can get together on land, but you will no longer be able to return to the sea. A merman cannot impregnate a siren. There are no half-breeds or mixes with sirens. A siren is made from the sea. Does that answer any lingering questions on that subject?" We all nodded.

As the sun started to rise, I remembered sitting on an island with Lachlan, and felt a small pang in my chest. I think I missed him.

"So why do we drown sailors?" Raidne asked. Thank you! I'm glad someone asked.

"Well, the sea is a living, breathing thing. She has a mind and a soul. To keep order and keep the sea alive and teeming with life, we must provide her with the means to do it. She doesn't like to take life, but she must do so to create new life." She paused for a moment. "At least, this is the story I've been told."

"Are we free?" asked Nixie.

"Free?" Cordelia repeated.

"Yes, like free to leave, to be in the sea's service elsewhere, like Raidne?" She pointed to the other siren.

"Oh, Well I suppose you are free to leave the city. But to remain in the city, with food and rooms and such from the merfolk, you must be a part of the Royal Choir in Aquacity. We do this to keep the numbers high and share the guilt. Also, we can teach you songs." My ears perked up with that.

"What do you mean 'teach you songs'?" I asked.

"Well, I guess you haven't noticed, but a siren can only sing a song they've learned from another siren. They can't create their own songs.

Each song has a purpose: distraction, temptation, sadness, mania, lust. We sing them into their deaths by altering the wave patterns in their brains."

"Wait ... is that why we can't talk or sing underwater, our voices alter brains?" "Precisely!" Cordelia clapped. "Although, someone's voice did ring out underwater," her eyes narrowed as she looked at me. "Have you made any other noises with your voice underwater?

I was tempted to say yes, but something pulled me back.

"No. I was having a nightmare." I decided a half-truth was the case and would have to be very careful. Cordelia looked lost in thought but clasped her hands together.

"Welcome to the choir, ladies. The other girls and I are going to sign the Lullaby of Woe, which would lure a man to throw himself overboard. Join in when you have the feel of the song, and we will get you ladies all brought up to speed and on your way through your service." She smiled and portrayed an air of 'nice leader type', but there was something nagging at the back of my mind. Maybe my trust had been broken one too many times.

The song was melancholic, and easy to learn. I picked up on it right away. I joined in late though, just listening to the different voices and picking out how they flowed into each other. At least two girls were singing the wrong parts for their voices. The harmonics could be better and fuller with some slight changes.

I joined in with their song, and that's when things got weird. I slotted myself into the middle of the mezzo-soprano portion. My voice intertwined with the other ladies, and I opted to fill the spaces that needed to be filled.

Then there was a giant splash. A whale swam near, then another splash as a pair of dolphins jumped out of the water and landed there. I stopped singing, pausing to look at the creatures who swam up to our island.

I swam out to the creatures, and decided I wasn't going to be afraid.

"Um, Cordelia, I thought the scream was supposed to keep the creatures away." Maya asked politely.

"It is," she said.

"Her scream could make my ears bleed if I had any," said the dolphin.

'Philip?' I asked, and the dolphin looked up, his eyes trained on me.

"Can you - can you understand me" he asked.

"I can understand you." He flipped back and shouted something incoherent. Then the whale asked, "Can you hear what I'm saying?"

"Yes. Am I not supposed to be able to understand you?" Phillip the dolphin was chattering away with the other dolphin. Cordelia called out, "Sahara, are you alright? I'm going to scream again to send the animals away." There were three "NOs" that came from the animals, and I called out,

"No, don't scream! Give me a minute and I can send them away myself."

"Alright guys, I have no idea how you came this close, but you have to go." I whisper-shouted at them. "We came because we were called by the song." The other dolphin said, but they started to swim away.

"Hey Red, meet me near Echo Island at sundown" Phillip said. "I think you are someone very special. DONT TELL ANYONE ELSE." Then he flipped and swam off. "How peculiar." Cordelia said, but her eyes were trained on me. Something behind them said she wasn't happy about being told no.

That evening, after all the sirens had gone to their rooms, I snuck out. I tried to find my own way outside, but I ended up lost.

That's when I ran into Namiko. I thought for sure I was in trouble. But she just looked at me and signed "leaving?" with a genuine smile on her face.

"Yes, but I'm lost. Help?" She nodded and gestured for me to follow her.

She showed me the way, leading out of the colosseum, and toward the channel. The place wasn't really guarded, just not exactly user friendly.

We reached the jellyfish door and pushed through. Good grief, it still hurt.

"Is that ever not painful?" I asked out loud.

Namiko looked at me and looked back at the door. My voice echoed in the water.

"I have no idea how you speak underwater. No other siren can." She responded. "But no, it always hurts. Where are you headed?" She asked. Now she just helped me out, and she knew I could speak, and she wasn't calling out in alarm or calling for a guard to tackle me, but I wasn't sure whether I could trust her.

"Uh" I stalled. She shook her head.

"I know. I'm sorry, I didn't want to drag you down here. I ... I ... I didn't have a choice. " She looked back behind her at the city and played with her hands.

"I'd like to try and make it up to you if I can. I know you might not trust me."

"Echo Island. Take me to Echo Island". She halted and stared at me, her eyes getting big.

"I'll take you!" she said and started to swim.

"I mean it. I, I, I can't tell you why exactly I didn't have a choice, but I didn't want to harm you. If there's anything Kai and I can do?"

"Kai?" I asked, surprised.

"Oh. I'm sorry. He is sorry too. He is being coerced, too. "

"Okay. okay. Stop apologizing. Let's get near the island."

"It's just ahead, but I see that there are some other animals around."

"That's what I'm hoping for. Philip told me to meet him."

"Wait? You understand the animals?" She asked, surprised.

" Yes. Surprise number two, not only can I talk underwater. I can hear and talk to the animals."

"You really are different. I wonder if ..." but she trailed off.

"Lass! You made it!" The Scottish accent had my heart racing instantly. I eagerly swam up towards the seal. But I saw the female seal was with him. Then a dolphin materialized, with a group of other dolphins.

"Shall we take this above water, where the sea can't listen?" He asked.

The group of us broke the surface and headed toward land.

I didn't know how my body would react, but once I hit the sand, and lifted my legs they split apart. I was able to walk. My dress clung to my legs, and it felt so weird to be on land. But so good. I sunk my toes into the sand and wiggled them, enjoying the sensation.

Namiko smiled at me, "Surprise number three" she said. I looked down, Oh right. Yeah, sirens aren't supposed to be able to change form.

Lachlan and Aerwyna took their skins off and stood naked on the shore. Namiko was sporting a set of black shorts and a pink tube top.

The dolphins popped up on shore and lifted their skins. My mouth must have dropped.

I heard a chuckle

"Aye, I remember you freaking out about my naked body, but you didn't stare at me like that. I'm a little jealous." I blushed a scarlet deep enough that it matched my siren skin.

He burst out laughing, and Aerwyna joined him.

The group of dolphins walked towards the sheltered screens. They picked through the buckets and threw on some shorts and dresses. Namiko stayed by the beach and was waiting kind of awkwardly.

"What's going on, Namiko? Are you going to join us?"

She looked at the sea and back and appeared to be nervous.

"I'm not supposed to be here." There was loud laughter from the center of the isle. "I should be back home ..." She looked outwards when we both saw a head pop out of the water. I braced for a shriek or cry of alarm when Namiko smiled.

"Kai! You got my signal!" She waved him in.

Kai waved back and came ashore, his tail turning into a set of teal shorts and legs. *Huh. Guess it's something with mermaids.*

"Hey Nam, what's going on?" And then he registered that I was there with her.

"You, you have legs?" He stammered.

"Surprise?" I said back to him. He looked at Namiko and she just shrugged.

"The dolphin shifters and selkies asked to meet her here."

"And I got lost trying to get out of the colosseum, and ran into Namiko-"

"And I sent you the signal and showed her the way. The shifters are all at the shelter."

"Please tell me there's enough shorts. I hate having to see a dolphin dick."

"They are all at least partially covered, but you know Phillip." Namiko smiled.

We walked back to the shelter where they were laughing loudly, and it almost appeared like a beach party. They had found bowls and glasses and empty shells to drink from and were playing around and tossing random items they found at each other.

"Dolphins have so much energy. Can I borrow some sometime?" Aerwyna's voice carried across the beach.

"Ah, Sahara, you've come! You should try a different dress. A dry one perhaps." She pulled out a white sundress from the bin of clothes and tossed it at me.

"Aye Lass, that one is looking a little … soggy." He looked me up and down and smiled.

"Not all of us have magic jewelry that provides clothes." Aerwyna looked pointedly at Kai and Namiko. Namiko fiddled with a ring on her finger I hadn't noticed before, and Kai sheepishly pointed at his earring stud. *Huh.*

"You'd have to ask Samudra for them. But she doesn't give them to everyone." Namiko said.

"Hush. Don't say the witch's name. She's not exactly a welcome topic around here" Philip shushed her.

"Come sit, we'll start a fire here shortly. Ian and Aishj are getting some wood." And sure enough the two shifters walked up with a pile of wood and in a short time there was a fire going.

All eight of us were sitting on the sand around the fire and I've never felt so content to be on a beach. I dug my feet into the sand and marvelled at the feeling. I was sinking my feet further and further in when Philip said something that caught my attention.

"Has anyone seen or heard from Brooke in the last twenty years?" He was looking pointedly at Kai and Namiko.

"Brooke who?" I asked.

"Brooke is the last siren who walked on land," Philip said, "but we haven't seen her since she returned to the sea. "

"Last I got from the guards was that she was still in a cell under the palace." Kai said.

"Can you get in to see her?" Iain asked.

"What for? I have some connections in the guard, but they are limited." he responded.

"Why do you need Brooke?" Aerwyna asked.

"Lachlan and I have found ourselves in those cells before, back when we were trouble-makers. I'm sure we could get ourselves down there." she said.

"We thought Brooke was the one that was going to bring peace to the ocean. She was taught all the things from each shifter group. But with the squids and octopi waging war against each other, and sharks split down the middle for each side, merfolk have banished them from Aquacity until things calm down," explained Philip. "Brooke should be able to explain the whole situation to Sahara, since we have lost a few from our original circle." He looked around and nodded at each person.

"Um. I have a question. Well, questions. Many of them, in fact." Philip smiled and nodded at me to continue.

"Let's start with the obvious, what the hell am I?"

"A siren". All seven of them responded together. I was a little taken aback.

"Okay, so if I am a real siren, why can I do things other sirens can't? Like why can I speak underwater? And walk on land? And understand animals? And..." I trailed off as the dream of me swimming through sand struck me. I dug my feet further into the sand, and on thinking about the dream, my feet had started to change to the red hue that was now familiar.

"And why am I a bright red colour?" I finished.

Kai was the first to speak.

"Your scale colour is generally just random. Sirens are usually more earthy and ocean tones because when they go into shallow waters it's easier to hide and blend in with camouflage before completing the tasks. Mermaids generally don't come up to the surface. In fact, maybe like ten percent of merfolk ever even bother to go on land."

"Mermaids are bright and colourful to be attracted to one another." Namiko said as she smiled. "Those who go on land ask Sam..." Philip coughed. "Er ... ask the priestess for a piece of jewelry to blend in as human. Gravity is very hard on a mermaid learning to walk."

"So, I'm just randomly bright red. Great." I dug my feet further into the sand.

"Aye lass, but it's a beautiful bright red. You don't blend into the ocean at all, it's easy to find you." He winked and Aerwyna nudged him with her elbow.

"So, this Brooke person, siren, mermaid, cross species?" I raised an eyebrow. "She's the person who can explain stuff to me. So why did I meet you all here tonight?"

"Well. I'm afraid that if we tell you what we think, you may swim off and never come to help." Philip said

"Help? Help with what?" I looked confused.

"He thinks you're La Reigne." Kai said.

"Loraine? Who is Loraine? And would one of you please make some sense?"

"Not Loraine, La Reigne. It's the name given to the one in the prophecy, spoken by an ancient sea witch who passed on many years

ago." Philip explained.

"We thought that it was Brooke about twenty years ago, but that was a failure. She was different from the other sirens. too." I perked my ears and looked up at Philip.

"What is this prophecy and how do I meet Brooke? " I asked.

"Well, according to Kai, we'll have to get thrown in jail." Aisjh said

"Why is she in jail?"

"Because, uh." He fell short. And the silence was telling. It was because she was different, and no one knew what to do about her.

"Why are sirens treated like second class citizens?" I asked, aiming my question at the two mermaids.

"Loralei" they answered in unison.

"Oh, another name. How many characters are in this story?" I mused out loud.

"Loralei is the Queen of Aquacity." Namiko explained. "But Aquacity, merfolk and each shifter/animal group are supposed to be self-governed with ambassadors." She gestured to the selkies and dolphins sitting around the fire. "Loralei took control over Aquacity and all of its citizens, demanding she be treated as a queen. "

"And people just accepted it?!" I asked, confused.

"Of course not. That's why war has been waged. In the name of Aquacity, and other cities in the ocean, the shifter packs have been fighting over loyalties to different mermaids. Samudra has been helping Loralei. Sorry!" she exclaimed when Phillip coughed again. "They keep the division between species in check for their gain and force the others to do what is required." She looked at Kai who put a hand on her shoulder and nodded.

"The island where we found you, that is our - uh - hunting ground. So to speak. We are forced to find girls who can sing and bring them to Aquacity." The circle was silent as we watched Namiko, her voice wavered, and the tears were welling in her eyes.

"We tell the best singers to go to Araxia's school, so that she can mass drown the ones she teaches the songs to. They became sirens in the service of the Queen. And then they compete for choir spots to earn the queen's favour. She sends them on missions to lure sailors to their deaths and sink ships for their goods."

"Okay. But why are you helping?" I just stared at her.

"She has my sister in that school. Just staying on land. She's not allowed to go into the ocean. Or come out. Melody is the keeper. She keeps us in line and threatens us."

"Your sister?" I asked, perplexed. There was so much I didn't know

about this world. Kai was giving Namiko a hug, and then it dawned on me. "She's blackmailing you, too." I said to Kai. Then I looked around the circle, at the "ambassadors". "You're all being blackmailed into helping with this whole thing, aren't you?" They all murmured, but they didn't deny it. "Is she holding someone hostage to you all?" I asked.

"Yes. She is holding many hostages, and so we have made this circle, to try and free the stolen, and save the ocean." Aerwyna said. "We all have someone trapped on land." She sighed and leaned into Lachlan. I wondered who was lost to her, to him, to *them*.

"We are looking for La Reigne, to help us fight and get back our loved ones and return the ocean to the peaceful place it has been." Said Ian.

"I think you might be La Reigne." said Phillip. "We believe you will be the turning point for the ocean."

My mind reeled as I took in the information and then the intense pressure of their expectations. They thought I was their chosen one, their prophet, their saviour. I started to breathe really fast and felt my chest tighten. *This can't be real. I am nobody's saviour.* I calmly walked away from the fire, my white dress catching in the breeze. I dug my feet into the sand and thought about getting to the beach. I blinked, and the ocean was in front of me, and the group was way back there.

I stood at the edge of the beach, perplexed about how I had arrived here so quickly. I heard my name called in the wind, but I ignored it for now. I looked down at my feet, and I was even more confused. My feet were buried in the sand up to my ankles, and my shiny red scales were showing to my calves. I lifted my foot out to have a look, the scales shining in the moonlight. *Damn, I wish I could see better.* I thought and then my eyes clicked

and I had a red filter. My foot was slowly transform-
ing back to toes and skin, the webbing between them
shrinking. There was no real sensation, but I could tell
that my foot under the sand was still transformed. But
it was in the sand, and it wasn't a tail as it was in the sea.

I heard my name called again, but I didn't want to
talk to them just yet. I stuck my foot back into the sand
and started to walk away from the edge. My mind was
still teeming with thoughts about all the turmoil in this
world I had just joined. And this group, this weird group
of seven shifters thought I was this Lorraine person,
that could help bring peace to the sea. Two days ago, I
was afraid of water, and couldn't swim. Now they want
me to save all the species within the ocean? Are they
fucking crazy? I needed to get to the other side of the
beach. Away from them. But I didn't want to go into
the water yet. I thought of the opposite side of the isle
where Melody and Namiko had dragged me into the
water. I blinked, then walked, and soon I was there. But
this time, I felt the movement of the sand, like it was
carrying me there.

As I opened my eyes, I was indeed on the other side of
the island. I sat on the beach, letting my legs rest on the
sandy beach. I watched with my red vision as my legs
transformed before my eyes to scales, but they did not
stick together. I was able to keep them separate, nor did
I grow a fin from my feet. I heard a noise behind me and
looked up to see Lachlan coming near. I sighed as the

gorgeous half naked man came and sat beside me. He didn't say anything, just sat down in the sand beside me. My heart beat a little faster, and then I wasn't thinking about the crazy story, and the people who were being blackmailed. But I thought of my dad and my friends, missing me at home.

I was taken from my family, and I hadn't been able to contact them. To tell them I'm not dead. My poor dad, who has now lost his daughter and his wife to the ocean. A tear slid silently down my cheek.

A warm finger reached up and wiped it away. He gave me a half smile and pulled me into a side hug. "I'm sorry, Lass." He squeezed but we just sat there. I enjoyed the salty smell from his chest, and I could hear his heartbeat as my head rested against him. My vision cleared from red, and my legs returned to my tan human skin.

I heard a sound behind me, and we both lifted our heads to look behind us. Namiko had come. "I'm sorry to interrupt, but we have about an hour before we have to get you back to Aquacity." She nodded at Lachlan and turned and walked back towards the shelter.

"Take your time, Sahara. Nothing is going to happen immediately." He said, "Phillip doesn't mean to have such high expectations of you." "No, it's okay. I was thinking about my dad, and how I'd feel if someone was holding him hostage and blackmailing me. I'd do anything, believe in anything, and work my ass off to

get him back. I wish I could just let him know I'm okay."
I hung my head.

"Let's check with Kai and Namiko about getting a call
to him." My head perked up.

'Wait, that's possible? He's deaf though, so it would
need to be a written message. I imagine all your com-
munication is monitored." He nodded and sunk his
head in thought.

"I just don't want him to hear that his daughter
drowned, like her mother. I trailed off.

"Your mother drowned?" He looked at me, and I
wasn't sure what to make of it. He stood up and held his
hand out to me.

I nodded. "She drowned when I was three years old."
"And your father is deaf?" He asked. I'm not sure what
he was insinuating, but I nodded.

"Was your father, by chance, a sailor?"

"Yes...?" He took my hand, and pulled me towards the
shelter, I followed, confused by whatever logic he was
asking. "Sahara, your mother didn't drown ..." he said,
and he took big strides towards the shelter. "What do
you mean my mother didn't drown?" I called after him,
running to catch up. He got to the shelter and held up
my arm, and announced,

"This is Brooke's daughter."

What?!

Six pairs of eyes stared at me. Lachlan was holding my arm up triumphantly, like I had won a match. I looked back at Lachlan and stared at him.

"What?" was all I could say, since my brain really wasn't working now.

"Your mother was the last siren to walk on land. She did so because she fell in love with a deaf sailor about thirty years ago. She was supposed to drown him but because he was deaf, he never succumbed. She saved him and fell in love with him. He could sign, and they could communicate. When Brooke and the sailor kissed, it was true love, and the sea gave her legs back. She lived on land with him for five years before she returned to the sea."

"Wait, you mean, Brooke had a child, with a human?" Phillip asked out loud.

"It would explain why she's so different. She's a product of the sea and the land." Aerwyna said.

"It explains the siren-like quality of your voice on land" Kai said.

"My mother's name wasn't Brooke, though." I choked, remembering the signature on my birth certificate, and the letter to my dad in my room.

"Was it Shannon?" asked Ian. I was taken aback. The only letter I had from her, and the swirling "S" that matched my own writing.

"It- It was" I whispered.

"Lachlan, you're right. This is Brooke's daughter. Brooke wasn't La Reigne, but her daughter is."

"Born of Land and Born of Sea. She is literally of both worlds." Aishj said.

"That's never happened before." Kai said.

"Kai, we need to see Brooke now more than ever." Phillip told the merman.

"I will need a few days to make arrangements."

"In the meantime, we need to go back to doing what we were doing. And not bring any attention to ourselves." He smiled at me.

"He wants you to try and pretend like you aren't different." Namiko said. "That means, no talking underwater. No talking to the animals in the water, and don't come up on land, unless one of us" she gestured to the seven of them "says it's okay. Getting found out will be a disaster."

"Not to mention, deadly."

I nodded. Kai looked up at the moon and sighed. "Nam, we've got to get her back. Cordelia will be up looking for them soon." She nodded and turned to the group.

"We'll meet back here in three days. I will try and get information from the sharks and see if they will join us."

"We will reach out to the squids" Ian said, pointing to the three dolphins who nodded.

"And we will talk to the octopi," Aerwyna said.

"Aye, the crazy bastards are going to murder us" Lachlan scoffed. Aerwyna nudged him and he smiled at her. A pang rang across my chest.

"Sahara, try and make friends with the sirens as best as you can. They are basically slaves to the Queen, so they might be interested in being freed. We will need all the help we can get," Namiko said. I smiled, and we all walked toward the beach.

Kai looked up again and sighed, "we've got to move fast. Sahara, I know the last time we pulled you; it was to force you. I'm sorry." He hung his head. "But can you let Nam and I pull you tonight? You're a slow swimmer still." He held out his hand as he walked into the water. Namiko smiled and held hers out as well.

"Don't let those fish tails tell you that you can't do it, Sahara," I heard Lachlan say. He had donned his skin and was the very cute seal waddling into the water, with Aerwyna close behind.

I smiled and grabbed the two outstretched hands and heard a bark behind me.

They pulled me under the water with them, and suddenly we were moving faster than I've ever moved before.

"Yeehaw!' I heard a shout and saw the dolphins racing beside us in the water. Namiko and Kai were moving faster than the dolphins and they were dragging my slow ass behind them. The click of yellow in my eyes let me see that we were already nearing Aquacity.

"I didn't think it was this close?" I asked out loud, forgetting that my voice echoed unnaturally in the waves.

"SHUSH" came the response from the dolphins, mermaids and selkies.

Since my arms were held by the two merfolk, I couldn't say a thing.

Lachlan swam up beside us and then waved farewell. They headed toward the south entrance, while Kai and Nam led me toward the East entrance. Through that damn jellyfish door again. ZZTT. Well, as fast as we went through, it didn't hurt as badly. We were already getting out of the channel when I realised we had gone in. Kai let me go then and smiled.

"Thank you for trusting me. I'm so sorry to have dragged you down

here. Namiko will get you to your court, and I'll distract the guards. Hopefully we will have a plan in a few days, so you can see your mother." Then he swam off and shouted at someone, as Namiko pulled me down the empty corridors.

"I will teach you the way, see the coloured corals on the corridors?" She said pointing at the tops of the arched hallway. "The siren court is on the far west of the colosseum; the yellow corals like to grow on the west side. The pink coral grows on the south, purple in the east, and blue green in the north. To leave the colosseum, follow the yellow to the blue green to the side entrance we used." The corals were blue-green and yellow mixed, and she pulled me down an all-yellow corridor. Then I saw the two guards ahead that were stationed in front of the Siren dorms.

We stopped and Namiko smiled and pointed. Kai was waltzing down the other side of the hallway singing.

"Hey! You, stop singing, the sirens are sleeping!" the guard on the right called out.

"Make me!" He sang "Row, row, row your boat, gently down the stream!"

"Get him out of here!" the guard called. Namiko pointed to a little alcove, "hide there, and then when they are both chasing us, go back to your room."

She swam out into the main hallway and joined Kai in the round. "Row, row, row your boat, gently down the stream, merrily, merrily, merrily, merrily, life is but a dream."

Kai and Nam taunted the guards a little more and they gave chase. I darted into the corridor and swam down the hallway. It was still quiet since no one was up. The guards had returned grumbling to themselves, saying "damn teenagers." I smiled and settled into the giant moss ball and lay my head to rest. *My mother was alive. And I was going to get to meet her.*

I could see shadows ahead. I tried to walk, but things around me shifted. I was underneath sand again. The shape ahead was wriggling and moving. It looked almost like it was swimming, I thought, maybe I should try to swim. I lifted my arm and kicked my legs. They separated and the sand flowed around me. I could feel the sand like it was fluid, allowing me to move through it. I kicked and swung my arms, and I was moving towards the shadow. It wriggled towards me, *my vision never becoming any clearer. I reached the creature, a crab tunnelling through the sand, but there wasn't a tunnel. The sand flowed around him and filled in behind him. He was swimming in the sand and so was I.*

I awoke to Maya shaking me. I swung my fist upwards, but thankfully missed her head. Her eyes opened wide as she realised I nearly hit her.

"Sorry" She signed sheepishly. "Cordelia woke me and told me to wake you. We need to go to the common area for food."

"Ok, I'll be right there." She smiled and swam out. I looked around the sparse room, the dream about sand still sitting heavily on my consciousness. I missed land so much. The sunny skies, the hot desert sand, the swing outside my porch. I missed my dad too, but my mother is still alive!

I wanted to know what I swam slowly down the corridor and saw a group of sirens sitting silently on the benches. Fruit filled the baskets floating on top of the water, and they were each chewing silently.

There were signings going on between them. They were engaged in full conversations and the longer I looked, the more animated the conversations became.

Signs about singing on the surface, about what they would do on land, about the food they would eat. I reached for a pear and sat on the bench beside Maya.

"Sorry for scaring you."

"It's okay. I'm OK. Any idea what's going on?" I asked.

Raidne swam up, a plum in hand, the juice dripping down her dark skin.

"I think we're doing something as a group," she signed. Pasha came into the room next, followed by Cordelia.

"Eat up. We have a ship today. The 5 new girls will join us today." She smiled at us, all sitting together. My stomach knotted up. I wasn't sure I wanted to know what it was that we were doing exactly, but the fanged smile from Cordelia and the other sirens had me on edge. Whatever it might be, it wasn't good.

Cordelia swam over and signed, "follow my directions and do what we say. We will sing the songs you learned yesterday." We all nodded. I was having a hard time swallowing, my pear sitting heavy in my throat.

We were led out of the colosseum by the two guards. We went from yellow coral to blue-teal and I tried to memorize the hallways we went through, but still got turned around. We were out of Aquacity and swimming fast. Maya and Raidne grabbed my hand and pulled me along, my swimming skills still terrible.

We slowed as we neared the surface. There was a large ship ahead in the distance. A cargo ship by the looks of it.

"Ladies. We will sing until this ship hits the rocks in those shallow waters. The sailors will dive into the water, and we give them no mercy. We shall devour their souls for the Sea, as she demands. The sharks will be by in time to help collect the debris and cargo for Aquacity."

My stomach flipped and I think I gagged. We were to sing these sailors to their death. I was going to be responsible for their deaths.

"Anyone not singing will be reprimanded. Which may include laying on the sand to bake until you turn to dust. Or locked in a cell under the palace until your time has been served, then eaten by a shark." One of the older, green-coloured sirens signed, her fangs gleaming in the light.

"I'm so hungry" one of the other ones signed. She looked like she was drooling, but the water hid the actual drool.

I looked at Maya and Pasha, but their eyes were wide too, shock filling their faces.

The other Sirens swam up to the surface, just barely breaking the surface and started a haunting tune. I recognized the tune. Cordelia swam over and pointed to Maya and I, "your turn, swim up and sing." Maya grabbed my hand and squeezed. I pulled her up and we swam together.

I felt my lungs empty of the sea water as we breached the surface. We each added our voices to the song, falling into a semi-circle on the starboard side of the ship, drawing it toward the shallows.

The tune was a beautiful haunting melody. I heard some shouts on deck and saw the big flap on the back of the boat turn. Pasha and Raidne surfaced as well, adding to the tune of melancholic seduction. Last to surface were Nixie and Cordelia, who completed the tune. The sound was ethereal to my ears, haunting, powerful, and enchanting. The ship steered hard right, aimed at the shallows. I saw a couple of shark fins break the surface behind the ship. My voice carried the tune. I was harmonizing with Maya, but Cordelia swam up. "Go higher" she signed. Higher was in the soprano range, a stretch for my voice, but I can sing that high.

I lifted my arms above the water, lifted my chin and reached for the higher octave.

She matched me, dropping a third and harmonizing. The sound was crystal clear and echoed off the rocks, so it sounded like there were more of us, singing in a round. It was beautiful, and I saw the boat listing into the shallows and snagging on the loamy ground. I heard some shouts from above and then heard a splash. A sailor had jumped in.

Cordelia's eyes shone with a frenzied look as the sharks circled closer. We shifted from the right side to behind the ship, never stopping the tune. We moved to the left and I watched in amazement as the deck filled with sailors looking at the ocean.

I tried to see their faces, but I couldn't.

Splash. Another sailor had jumped and was paddling in the water, headed towards a small group of sirens. One ducked under the water and met him, pulling him under. There was a soft gurgle, barely noticeable above our song.

Then the water around the sailor slowly turned a crimson red.

Splash. Splash. Splash. A few more sailors jumped in. One by one the sirens ducked into the water and pulled them under. The sailors were jumping in groups now, as the ship teetered, threatening to capsize them all.

Cordelia's fangs were elongating in her mouth. The sharks swam closer and I could hear them.

"Mmm, fresh meat tonight."

"Circle to the left, boys, once the sirens get them off the ship, it's a free for all."

"I can't wait" and one shark took off for the group that just dove in.

The smell was like rusted nails had been jammed into my nostrils. Cordelia stopped signing and shouted, her voice screeching and shrill, but carrying a frenzied lust.

"Drag them under and rip their throats out. Make sure no sailor survives. FOR THE SEA!"

"FOR THE SEA!" the other sirens shouted. I looked at Maya, at the crazy look in her eyes and saw the bloodlust there. Pasha and Raidne had already sunk below the waters.

I treaded water, feeling sick to my stomach as I watched the water change from blue to red to black. There was no one left on the surface, so I let myself sink into the iron filled water. The tang that hit my mouth made me gag, and I gasped as I saw the silent underwater scene.

The sirens were whipping through the waters, slashing the throats with their long, clawed fingers. I looked at my own hands and stared at the sharp curled hooks. I could hear the gurgles and the bubbles as the sailors expelled their last breath of air. Several of the older sirens were ripping out the throats with their sharpened teeth, their faces coloured crimson, as they tossed the fallen sailors down into the sea.

Around the sirens the sharks were taking part in the bloodlust with their teeth shredding the skin and tearing into flesh and bone. I saw Maya grab a sailor who was trying to swim to the surface and yank his leg down. She lifted her hand and slashed four gashes across his face. His eyes were dimming, and Maya's eyes were frenzied, yellow and large. The smile that flashed across her face as she squeezed his throat made me shudder. She dug her thumb into his neck, and even under the water, the blood spurted, and he let out his breath. His lungs filled with water and his last breath gone as she leaned into his chest and bit down, tearing out his windpipe.

It was fast, vicious, and violent. The sharks and sirens had dispatched every sailor on the ship. They dragged the bodies to a deeper part of the sea. The body parts the sharks hadn't eaten were sinking into the dark abyss, a watery graveyard of men who fought valiantly for their lives. They never stood a chance. I watched, transfixed and unable to move or turn away. I was disgusted and wanted nothing but to retch and swim far, far away. I had caused those sailors to sail the ship into the shallows. I caused them to jump into the water. I was responsible for their deaths. This can't be what the sea wants … is it? I slowly swam to the surface and stared at the water surrounding me. The carnage and chaos. There were clothes, hats, and some loose limbs that decorated the scene. The murky water was a mess of red, blue, and dark purple hues. I lifted my head out of the water and swam towards the shallows where the ship was stuck. I wanted nothing more than to get away from these monsters.

I heard a sound behind me as a shark swam nearby.

"Didn't join the frenzy?" he said, his tone breathy, as if he were physically exhausted. "What a waste." He swam away, back to the scene of chaos.

I pulled myself onto a rock and curled my arms around my legs. I couldn't be a part of this. This was cruel, disgusting, horrible. The stench of blood and salt hit my nose. I gagged and tears filled my eyes. The other new girls had not hesitated, tearing into their throats with gusto. They were filled with a lust that I could not feel. A desire, no, a need to tear into flesh and taste it.

Cordelia surfaced above the water and gave a shriek that echoed in my ears.

"Capsize the ship, we need to tip the cargo into the sea." The group of sirens and sharks surrounded the ship and pushed, pulled and forced the ship back into the sea, the gaping hole on the right-side filling with rushing water. The ship was unbalanced, awash with sea water, and sinking fast. They tipped it over so it was on its side, falling into the dark.

Once the ship rested on its side in shallow waters, they swam in and out, collecting the cargo. It appeared to be random items. I swallowed my nerves now that the sea was back to blue. The debris appeared to be random merchandise - toys, jewelry, kitchenware, clothing - cluttering the area. Maya swam up and nudged me. She appeared to have returned to normal.

"Are you okay?" She asked. I didn't respond. I was not okay. I was anything but okay. This wasn't okay. We just sent a boat load of people to their deaths for junk. For what reason? For what purpose? As tears filled my eyes, I shook them away. "Time to go, sharks, the merfolk are near." I turned my head to watch the sharks dip down into the water and swim off, looking for the merfolk.

Cordelia shrieked, the piercing cry hurting my ears. She called the sirens to return to the beaches from yesterday. About a dozen Merfolk swam up carrying bins and equipment. They swiftly attached it to the cargo bins and dragged it away, as we swam off.

Perplexed, I wondered what was going on. We sank a ship for the merfolk, killed all the sailors and let the sharks feast, and then the merfolk stole the goods, so they could ... what, sell it back to the humans? We're merfolk pirates? If that was true, why wouldn't they take the ship and sail the merchandise to a port for sale?

And it dawned on me, they were creating a shortage of items. Items lost at sea, so they could flood the markets later.

We neared the beach where we practiced yesterday. Cordelia and the older sirens lounged against the rocks, looking peaceful and serene, the crimson stains washed away with the saltwater swim.

I lay against the beach underwater, just listening to the chatter.

"Did you see the way I slashed the two together?" "I managed to slit a throat and bite through one at once. It was exhilarating."

"Blood in the water makes me feel so alive."

T he rest of the day was a blur. Cordelia had us practice singing. They talked and signed about how
much they loved the hunt. I just tried to survive the
ordeal.

We were brought back to the colosseum, and I barely
felt the jellyfish door. My mind was numb. I remember
reaching the common room and pulling a mango from
the floating baskets and quietly sitting, chewing it.

No one bothered me, too excited in their own minds. Maya eyed me curiously but didn't interrupt. Once the older sirens had gone off to their rooms, I followed and laid down on my moss bed.

I stared at my clawed fingers, wishing I could rip the claws out. My red scales captured the light from the glowing algae, and it danced in my room. Thank God there wasn't a mirror. I didn't want to see into my own eyes or to see the face of the murderer looking back at me.

I hadn't joined the frenzy. I hadn't felt the need. It was something perverted and unnatural. It made my heavy heart sink lower in my chest and I felt like retching again.

My eyes would have been filled with tears if I were not underwater, but it did nothing to dispel the feeling of needing to cry.

I wanted to sob and wail and break down. Those were people. Real humans. People like my father, working to support their families. They had people waiting for them. Waiting for them to return home.

I sat up and hiccupped, unable to stop the heaving coming from my body. I needed to puke. I needed to spit up bile and blood and guilt, but the water held it in. The water surrounded everything in me, and I wanted to pluck my scales from my skin, I wanted to peel off the red skin and drown in the salt water I was breathing.

I heard a small knock on the door and Maya slowly swam in. She looked at me as a hiccup escaped. Her yellow eyes reflected my face, and I saw my own yellow eyes, sagging and hollow, staring back at me. But I also saw the hurt and guilt in Maya's eyes.

"Do you feel guilty, too?" She signed and her body language said so much more than the words ever did. I nodded, and she swam up and sat on the moss bed next to me.

"I've never done anything like that. There was a pull in me I've never felt. It was like a monster in my head had been unleashed and took control. I remember feeling guilty, and afraid, and then I was a horrible monster, ravenous and hungry for blood. I killed so many sailors." She hung her head in shame, and her blue scales flushed with a purple flash.

"How did you stop yourself?" She asked me. "I tried to stop, but it overpowered me." I looked at her and grabbed her hand and squeezed.

"I didn't have any blood lust. I didn't feel any urges, other than to run and retch. But I know the others felt it. No one was able to overcome it." I told her. "It's not your fault." And then I hugged her.

I heard another tap at the door as Pasha and Raidne swam in, eyes swollen and downcast. They too looked guilty and crestfallen.

"Is this what our life is now?" Pasha asked.

"Drowning sailors and gutting them alive for sport?"

"I can't do that again" Raidne signed, settling beside us on the moss bed. "I feel sick."

"Did everyone feel a sense of doom and intense hunger?" Maya asked.

The other two nodded, and they shared a moment. Maya reached for Pasha and pulled her into a hug. Raidne swam over and grabbed Nixie, bringing her into the room.

"Let's all stay together tonight." Raidne signed. "I'm going to see their faces in my nightmares."

Me too, I thought. But the five of us cuddled together on the moss, each wallowing in our own guilt and loss of control. The girls had succumbed to whatever monster was inside, but me? I had succumbed to being passive. I stood by and watched it happening and did nothing.

I hugged each of my friends and felt a need to protect them. There was nothing normal about this if they all felt as sick as I did.

They feel guilt and remorse, and they don't deserve it.

If I am Lorraine or whatever that prophecy thing is, maybe I can help. Maybe I can keep the humanity alive in these girls before they succumb to the monster inside.

I wouldn't be able to do it alone. I didn't even know what I needed to do to change this. The answer could not be 'nothing'.

I can't be passive, letting people die, because someone else said to do so. Two more days until I can talk to the group. Do they have a code name? A secret group for peace within the ocean. A group of creatures who had been wronged by the people in power, who stand to lose everything if we don't fight back.

Maya's head was resting on my lap now, her breathing even and tempered through the gills on her neck. She was resting, but her face was twisted.

She will be haunted by the memories of those sailors; those lives she personally sent to the depths of the sea.

I whispered quietly "Is this what the sea really wants?"

The next day we did not down a boat, thankfully. But we were called to Siren Isle to have a chat with the other sirens. They asked us how we slept, whether the sailors had satiated our hunger. The five of us played along, desperately agreeing to anything to make them stop talking about the event,

"What happens to the cargo?" I asked, trying to change the conversation.

Cordelia's eyes flashed, and she shook her head.

"That's need-to-know information. You're still new here, Red, and quite frankly, I don't trust you."

Fair. I am new. And there was a good reason not to trust me.

Then came the surprise. Cordelia called out, screaming away any hint of animals, and then spoke.

"We will be meeting with Samudra for jewelry for the new sirens, as congratulations on the successful take-down of their first ship."

Wait, why would sirens get magic jewelry? They couldn't go on land. They didn't need magic clothes. So, unless Samudra dealt in other types of jewelry, I didn't know what the purpose would be. What could she trade a siren?

How am I going to hide my special behavior? How am I going to react to this highly regarded Sea Witch? Then came the low blow.

"Tomorrow night, we will be performing for Queen Loralei. A celebration for her fifth year as the reigning monarch of Aquacity. We will perform in the palace, with all of the sea's ambassadors.

"Can we perform something new?" I asked. "The same songs seem so simple, and they all tend to have malicious intent."

"Different songs? Sirens can't compose or create their own music." *The hell they can't,* I thought. "We can only sing the songs the Sea has given us." One of the older sirens said, shaking her head. Cordelia cut us off.

"We will meet with Ashera later this afternoon in the palace. We are to prove that we can be trusted." She looked at me, solidifying the fact that I stood out as untrustworthy.

I blinked back at her, trying to seem unperturbed.

Pasha and Raidne seemed to grow excited. "We get to go to the palace!"

"We get to see the queen!"

Maya stared at me, her expression blank. She seemed lost in thought.

I tapped her shoulder. "Is something wrong?"

She shook her head. "No, it's just a feeling that something isn't right. Plus, I really don't like Ashera, she's kind of mean towards the sirens who aren't good enough for the Royal Choir."

"What happens to the sirens who didn't make the choir?" I asked.

"Before I was taken to the colosseum for auditions, we were held on a donut-shaped island. Ashera runs the island. Merfolk find new sirens who have been born by the sea and drag them to the isle. We are trapped there since we can't cross land like merfolk.

They don't treat us … poorly, per se. But we're told to practice singing until we can pass the audition. Then we will have freedom to serve the sea correctly."

There's another island of sirens.

"How many more sirens?" I asked her.

"There were about fourteen of us living out there when we were selected to audition." She shrugged. There were fourteen others held captive. Completely at the mercy of the merfolk. I shuddered as I thought. Those girls had pledged their service to sea, and then were trapped in something they never knew existed.

I looked at the four girls with whom I had formed a friendship. Knowing there were others made my stomach hurt again. I wanted to help them, but how?

"Alright, ladies, Ashera will be bringing us up to speed about palace etiquette. Although it's basically, do nothing unless you are told to." Cordelia signed. "Here she comes now."

Sure enough a golden yellow tail flicked the water in the distance. I sank down into the water and let my vision yellow over. It dulled her tail and bronze skin and made it manageable to see her. Also being underwater reminded me to keep my mouth shut, since Ashera was obviously employed by the queen and kept the sirens in line. Although Donut Island sounded delicious - I miss donuts - it also sounded oppressive and was essentially another prison for these girls.

"Good afternoon, Royal Choir." I heard Ashera say.

"Congratulations to the newly selected bunch. Nixie, I'm proud you finally made it this time.

"I'm here to escort you into the Queen's palace for a test run, since we need to ensure there will be enough air for your lovely voices to echo and reverberate just right. We also want to ensure that the performance will go according to plan." Her voice was high and peppy, much different from the voice I recalled in the jellyfished room below the audition. But it was false, trying to lure us into a sense of security and wellbeing.

"Please, follow me back down through the city. The very center is where we are headed. Watch for the guards. Do not engage with anyone in the city, do not do anything unless you are asked to by a guard or myself. Understood?" She looked at each one of us.

We all nodded yes and followed her down to the city.

This time we entered through some jellyfish doors on the south of the city, toward the ocean floor. Two guards stood by, monitoring the flow of traffic. They acknowledged us, but only just.

We arrived at the center of the palace and swam in through the front doors. It felt very surreal. The building itself was constructed of dark marble, but coral was growing from every surface imaginable. The corals were in every colour of the rainbow. There were paths, where the seafloor was covered with sand, but the coral formed tunnels and archways. We followed several of these, and then we dipped down low, and then straight up. It reminded me of a toilet drain, and when we surfaced, I understood why.

In the middle of the grand palace was a huge air pocket.

The walls were stone, and seaweed hung down from the damp ceilings. Stalactites and stalagmites completed the beautiful cavernous room. Beach sand ran about a third of the way out, making it seem like we were entering from a giant lake. On one side of the cavernous room, there was a throne carved from crystal. Glowing algae filled the roof with a blue glow that reflected off the water's surface. It was a beautiful room.

As Ashera led us over to the right side of the room, a woman walked onto the beach from an attached room. Her long beautiful white hair hung loose from her head down to her stomach. She was wearing a lovely royal blue slip dress that clung to her every curve, and a crown with blue sapphires adorned her head. She stopped at the edge of the water, and beckoned Ashera over. Ashera told us to stay where we were on the right-hand side of the cavern.

Ashera's golden tail split into two dark skinned legs, and a golden slip dress that sparkled in the algae's light. She walked calmly up to the woman in blue and dipped her head. I couldn't hear what they were saying, but it wasn't long before Ashera was returning to the water. She swam back over to us, and the woman turned and disappeared into the room off the side.

"Ladies, that was Queen Loralei. You are never to utter a word in her presence, other than to sing when asked. Understand?" We all nodded. "This is the chamber. When we sing tonight, there will be a bridge placed from that wall" she pointed to the far eastern wall," to the edge of the beach. We will be on this side and we are to sing so that the whole room can hear. ""This room will be filled with all kinds of mammals and sea creatures tonight, but you are the entertainment. No talking, and only sing when told. Which is right now. Cordelia, please begin the Lull. "

Cordelia proudly swam up front and began to sing with her hauntingly beautiful voice. The echo and reach were exquisite. The other girls began to join in, and I couldn't help but get lost in the sounds as I joined the choir. Then Ashera gave us a cue to stop.

"Very good. You all sound great. This will be good. Follow me down below to the holding chamber."

The holding chamber was a small underwater cavern lit up by more algae. There were fish swimming in and out, and a couple of the older girls grabbed them and bit into them. I guess it was food. There was some soggy fruit. We entertained ourselves with idle chit-chat signing back and forth. Asking each other what kind of ceremony it would be, and whether the queen would even acknowledge us. I felt like I was back to performing onstage.

Much later, Ashera returned and brought us back up the drainpipe. The room had been transformed. There was a glass bridge settled into the eastern wall, and it led all the way to the beach. There were all kinds of animals and shifters on the beach and in the water. Octopi, squids, sharks, serpents, dolphins, seals, and mer-folk were all around the room. I noticed a few guards positioned at key locations both above and below the water. On the beach were human forms, carrying skins of whatever sea animal they were. I noticed Lachlan and Aerwyna, standing off to the far left of the beach, and Phillip and Aishj were not far from them. There were many others I didn't know. I hadn't known the ocean held so many creatures who were half human, or human formed.

When we raised our heads out of the water the room quieted, and the creatures in the water lifted their heads out in anticipation. Queen Loralei stood on a dais formed of coral and crystal. She raised her arms.

"Welcome to all. The Sea sends her warmest wishes, and I am proud

to be your queen for these last five years."

"LONG LIVE QUEEN LORALEI!" came a chorus of shouts from

the room.

"Thank you, thank you," she smiled and paused as the room settled back. "I have been a fair and just queen, trying to return peace to our world and culture, but there are groups who are not happy about my reign and have decided to wage war outside of Aquacity's domed walls. This breaks my heart. I want us all to get along."

"Then quit killing my kind!" Came a shout in the wa-ter, there were guards there quickly plucking an octopus out of the water and dragging him to the beach. I looked at the other sirens and Maya signed "what happened?" I forgot that they couldn't understand the animals.

"He said she was killing his people," I signed back.

"Oh" she mouthed but then watched the scene. "My darling, Octavius, whatever do you mean? I have killed no one.

But what you say is traitorous, and an outright lie." Loralei said."You send the merfolk, the sharks, and the dolphins out to attack us. Our numbers are dwindling because you continue killing them. My family and my friends are being hunted." "No. They aren't. They are being sought out to bring peace to our beloved section of the sea. Your kind persist in attacking our search parties. And so, we must defend ourselves against these ruthless attacks."

She pointed to the guard. "Strip his skin." The guard obliged and pulled off the skin ruthlessly. A naked man fell to the beach, swearing as he tried to stand with dignity.

"I will not be gaslit, you wretched mermaid bitch." He ran towards the standing woman, but the guards grabbed him, and forced him to his knees, pinning his arms behind his back.

"I am a fair Queen. I will give you a chance to go free. "She gestured to the bridge. "You must cross the bridge over the waters to the east wall while my siren choir is singing. If you make it to the end, you will be free to leave Aquacity. If you jump into the water, you will serve fifteen years in my sand holding cells." Octavius the Octopus balked at the offer. "That's ridiculous, no one can resist the Siren's call!"

"Very well. We will start with one siren. For each one you resist, I will take off one year. If you make it to the far side, before all of them are singing, you are free." She looked around, getting nods of approval from the creatures around her. I watched as Lachlan and Aerweyna stared blankly ahead, making no motion to stop it. Why wouldn't anyone stop this?

The guards stood him up and dragged him up the glass bridge. He looked at the far eastern wall. I estimated that the bridge must have been about a mile long, and even a quick runner would take some time to cross it.

Ashera pointed at Cordelia, "Start singing." She began the lull and the man was released from the guards. He started to run. I watched in morbid curiosity as the naked man sprinted for his life trying to cover his ears.

Ashera pointed to the girls one at a time in intervals. There were three singing when she pointed at Nixie, and the man faltered on the bridge. He was only about a third of the way. He stopped running, and lowered his hands, He stared into the water. Ashera pointed at Maya, and she harmonized with Cordelia. The man stared at the sirens, tears in his eyes, and jumped. Ashera signalled to cut the song.

'Five sirens, five years taken off! Ten years for your sentence then. Guards take him to the sand cells. We will keep his skin separated for now." Her smile was wicked, and her voice was filled with excitement. The room erupted with clapping and cheering. "Our Fair Queen" was chanted by a group.

My mouth open, eyes wide, I couldn't believe what I had just watched. We weren't brought in as entertainment. We were brought in to deal sentences before they even received a fair trial.

"Bring out the shark!" The wicked one they called Queen ordered. Two guards dragged out a naked woman with a cropped haircut. She was fighting them, but they held fast. There was a sickening pop that echoed as her arm was wrenched from her socket and the woman's scream made me cover my ears. They then stomped on her leg, bringing her to her knees.

"Clara, you stand accused of espionage. You have been seen relaying sensitive information to the octopi and sharks that continue to fight against the peace I would bring to the sea." Loralei continued, oblivious to the woman's pain.

"For the crime of coming into my court and pretending to be a warrior who pledged her loyalty to me, and then turning into a traitorous bitch." She sneered as the guards forced her to her feet. "You too will walk the bridge to the east wall. Should you make it, you are free to leave my court and never return. Your skin, however, remains in my custody for the next twelve years. One year for every time you were seen passing information."

Ashera pointed to us and whispered, "Get ready to sing."

"You know," the queen mused loudly, walking off the dais. "I quite enjoyed seeing how many siren calls they could make before succumbing. Let's do that again." She smiled as the audience clapped and cheered.

Ashera nodded and pointed to Nixie. "You begin with 'The Call.'" That song, as far as I understood, was a little more entrancing than the lull. It was a beckoning, instead of a slow lullaby that hypnotized the one being called.

Nixie sang beautifully, and Clara, the shark, held her arm awkwardly and started to hobble down the bridge. The octopi, squids and merfolk were booing her, while the sharks looked on in solemn silence. Something seemed off with the sharks. Why were they just watching? Someone must do something to help! This couldn't be the way the courts are handled in the ocean, could it?

Ashera pointed to Raidne next, and then Pasha, By the time Pasha had joined Clara had stopped the forward momentum and was straining to hold onto the bridge railing with her good hand. Her broken arm was hanging awkwardly, and as soon as Ashera pointed at me, she jumped over.

I was momentarily relieved, since I didn't have to sing, but the relief was short-lived when the sharks in the water immediately swarmed their downed kin and tore her to shreds. The scream was short, and the blood in the water made my stomach queasy.

"Well, that was a surprise clean up. Not wanting to watch her be tortured in a sand prison then." The Queen laughed, but even the audience wasn't cheering as loudly as they had for Octavius' fall. "We have one final traitor to deal with. However, this one will need to be handled … differently." She paused and looked towards us. "This is why I brought the entire Siren Choir to perform tonight." She gestured to her guards in the water and brought up a siren. I blinked; she looked familiar but was not part of the choir. It was one of the sirens from the auditions who didn't make it. Number one. The one who just screamed her protest. I looked at Maya, signing "what the hell is going on?" Maya shrugged back at me. Cordelia was being held back by the other older sirens; hand clamped over her mouth.

"This siren decided that our Siren Sanctuary on Donut Island was not good enough. She was trying to rally up the rest of the sirens to figure out a way out through the sand." The queen laughed. "As if a siren could make it across the sand before her tail dried out, and she turned to dust. But this one tried. She even convinced a few others, and now they are dust on the beach." A few more sirens covered their mouths in disgust. They had lived with those girls, but I hadn't. Even

Ashera looked a little shaken up and was trying to keep her composure.

The guards dragged the angry siren above the water, and she screamed. The piercing noise was enough to make me and everyone in the room cover their ears, except the Queen and her guards. They must have been wearing some kind of ear protection. The sirens all ducked under the water to drown out the piercing wail. But it was abruptly cut off. We rose back up and saw that the guards had stuck a knife up through the bottom of the protester's jaw.

I heard a cry out from us and saw Cordelia swimming away. "Constance! Nooo" She cried.

"Ah, so my Choir was in on the scam. Trying to cross the sands. Well today you will have your chance to make it up to me." She made a signal, and then we were surrounded by the guards.

They dragged Constance and Cordelia to the sand and laid them on it.

"You want to get across the sands and be free? You must cross from

the North side to the South side before you turn to dust. And my traitorous daughters," She looked at the rest of us. "You must all stay ashore, while they make the attempt." The audience gasped, and I could hear whispers across the room.

"She's going to kill the whole choir?"

"Sirens can't stay on land; they turn to dust"

"There is no way they were all a part of the attempt to flee."

"But why would they flee? The Queen wants peace, not war." The guards were now dragging us all to the shore. Lachlan and

Aerwyna were on the northern side and wore similar shocked expressions. I was going to be found out, but these girls were going to die. I tried to dive under, and flee the guard, but then I had an idea. I wasn't going to be passive anymore. They can't die because I didn't try.

"I want to cross the sands" I called out.

The room went silent, and the guards paused momentarily as they dragged the sirens ashore. Cordelia and Constance were on the shore, and they were drying off quickly. I needed to be sneaky and convince her to stay true to her word.

"We have a sacrifice?" She asked surprised. "Which siren dares to speak to me?" She looked around at the group, and the guards aimed their spears at us. I shrugged free of my guard captor and swam close to the shore.

"I do. I am Sahara. Do you swear on your honour that you will let us, that's all the Sirens, including Constance, be free of any charges, and free of Aquacity, if I can cross the sands? The entire length of the sands, from north to south."

"You're a brand-new siren. Have you even been out of the water since you arrived?" She scoffed." You won't even make it to the centre before you are a pile of dust. You're welcome to give it a try." She waved me away, and I caught Lachlan's eyes widen and he mouthed 'no'. Aerweyna elbowed him. I looked at the girls, expressions of fear and terror on their faces.

"DO YOU SWEAR IT?" I shouted at her.

"Yes, yes. I swear that if you make it across the sands I will let the sirens free."

"All of the sirens. They all go free."

"Fine. All the sirens go free." She acquiesced, and I swam towards the North shore. Lachlan and Aerwyna looked at me curiously, and I could see on their faces that they were worried. The guards dragged a crying Cordelia and the bleeding Constance into the water.

I could see all the sirens eying me, curious as to whether I could possibly save them all. The audience hushed, and I felt the room watching me. Maya had tears in her eyes, the silly girl couldn't hide her emotions. Raidne and Pasha just held solemn looks and Nixie was biting her nails. The older sirens hugged Cordelia and Constance, stopping her from bleeding out.

I was calm, I could do this. I would hit the sand, dry my legs and transform, then run across from this side to that side. She is duty-bound to keep her promise to free the sirens. She will not be pleased by the outcome, but that's to be expected. I sighed, dragging myself up on the shore.

My skin dried quickly, and I pulled my white dress down as I crouched waiting for the change. I heard some clapping, the older sirens, urging me to go.

"Shut them up!" I heard a shout, and the guards were pulling them under the water, where they would be muted. The Queen then took her first full look at me, eying me up and down, a sneer across her face.

"Very well, Sarah, or whatever your name is. You have until you turn to dust to get across the sands. I expect to be entertained. Begin."

I looked straight at her and smiled. I smiled at Lachlan, at Aerwyna, and at Phillip on the other side. When I stood on my changed legs, I heard a gasping sound from all over the room. I didn't bother to look. I started to run.

The sand slipped through my feet, pulling, and pushing, helping me along. I was gliding through the sand, moving faster than I ever had before, it was moving for me. I could hear the angry shouts, but I didn't care. I was going to free those sirens from this tyrant queen, and then I was going to find my mother and break her free. The sand carried me faster and faster as I moved my feet, kicking as if I was swimming. The south wall was looming before me, and I could hear the cries of astonishment, followed by "STOP HER!"

The guards were chasing me, but they were no match for my speed on the sand. The years of growing up in the desert, and a newfound connection to the sand, meant I could feel where they were. It was as if the sand was an extension of me. I dodged the guards, the mer-folk, and the shifters and ran until I hit the wall. There was a rock near the bottom of the wall. I picked it up and carved a large X across the corals and rocky facade. Then I turned and dove out into the water, turning back into my siren form, diving deep. The merfolk under the water were yelling at me, aiming spears at me, and I was surrounded. I rose back up to the surface. I held up my hands in surrender as Loralei stomped up the south side of the shore to confront me.

"You swore that the sirens would go free if I made it to the other side." I huffed. "I did what you asked. Let them go free."

"They have nowhere to go." She sneered. "And you aren't going anywhere. I swore that the *sirens* would go free. You are no siren. Take her to the sand cells." She turned, and then called back "And tie her hands and feet." She stomped back to the dais as the guards pushed me towards the shore. I obliged and followed the guards, getting sent to the sand cells meant I might be able to find my mother. I smiled at the wretched queen, knowing I had at least gotten a rise out of her.

"Take the sirens back to the colosseum now." She called out to Ashera.

"My Queen, are you not going to honour your word?" Phillip called out. "You gave your word that you would set those sirens free, and it is your word that we are relying on to maintain the treaty between the Merfolk and Dolphin Kin," he continued. Loralei blanched, as she realised that her treaties might be in jeopardy. Phillip smiled and winked at me as someone else joined him.

"Queen Loralei, the Dolphin Ambassador has a point. Will you go back on your word because it didn't please you?" Another shifter male asked her. Her face was flushing red as she turned and tried to come up with a response.

"I- I am the queen, and I am trying to keep the peace between the sea creatures."

"And the sirens were promised their freedom, by your mouth. Dolphin and Squid Ambassadors are both correct that you should honour your word, or we will also have to re-evaluate the agreements between our kin." She was turning purple now.

"She is not a siren, and tricked me into a contract with her," she huffed out.

"But are you a fair and just queen, as you say?" Another called out, and soon there were nods and calls for her to not go back on her word. Her lips were thin, and she grabbed at her crown with both hands, and called to the guards. "Release the sirens from Aquacity." Her voice was strained, as if she were fighting to get the words out.

"And the ones on Donut Island." Lachlan chimed in. "You gave your word; all of the sirens would go free."

"And so I did." she said through clenched teeth. The ambassadors were all wearing matching smiles of triumph. The queen returned to the dais and took a breath. I didn't hear what she was saying, as I was abruptly pulled into a crevice in the wall. The guards marched me through the palace walls, saying nothing. We marched for a while, and I grew dizzy and lost in the stonework and coloured corals. I didn't say anything, but I don't think it would have mattered.

We were now in a damp musky-smelling part of the palace and the walls were covered in slimy, green algae. The dark green glow was awful to see through with my human eyes, and I was trying to force my yellow eyes to click into place when I was shoved into a room. It was covered in bricks of sand. The guards grabbed some kelp and wrapped my arms and legs and left me in the middle of the sand room. Then there was the nasty red jellyfish stretched across the doorway. The greenish-yellow Jellyfish was painful, and the pink jelly in the colosseum was enough to keep the rest from touching it. This one must be excruciatingly painful.

I sighed as I sat on the cell floor, my feet digging into the sand. I concentrated on the sand and whether I could feel where things were like I did while I was dodging the guards. I hoped the sirens were okay. How did I go from a teaching assistant to negotiating for lives? I was so thankful that the ambassadors stood up and demanded that she follow through. What was I thinking? The adrenaline had worn off, and I faced the predicament I was in. I was in jail and underwater, incarcerated by a tyrant queen that I had just pissed off. In the process, I had demonstrated that I wasn't a true siren. What would happen to me now? How was I going to get out of this mess?

I heard a small gasp and looked up to see Kai's surprised face peering in.

"Sahara? What the hell are you doing in a cell?" he asked. I shrugged in my bindings and smiled at him.

"Well, I made a deal with that tyrannical blue bitch. She didn't like the outcome and claimed I wasn't a real siren, so here I am." He looked at me and shook his head. "What kind of deal did you make?"

"I ran across the sands and freed all the sirens from her control, before she could turn them all to dust?" His jaw dropped open, and he stared at me in wonder, then smiled. "That was kind of stupid. Very brave of you, but stupid."

"Says the man who pushed me off a cliff to try and kill me." His sheepish smile faded, and he looked back at me sadly. "I am sorry, Sahara. I didn't want to do it. Honestly." "I know, Kai. Clearly, there is a much bigger world out here. Now all jokes aside. I'm scared. I have no idea what they're going to do to me. Or what to do next. Also, what are you doing down here?"

"The ceremony is still going on, so my guard friend said this was the best time to get in here and find the one I need to talk to. So, I came looking for Brooke, and

I'm trying to map a way out. It's built like a maze down here."

"It wasn't just me getting lost then." I pulled my legs to my chest and wrapped my tied arms around them and rocked back against the sand. My feet dug into the sand, and I concentrated on that feeling I had while I was running. It was as if a new sensation had opened to me. I could map out where the sand was, the location of the cells and whether there was movement. I opened my eyes and looked at Kai, deciding to trust him.

"The sand tells me there are prisoners in the two cells across the hall, three empty cells, and the one at the end of the hall that sort of dips into water has someone in it. If Brooke is a siren who isn't turned to dust, I'd bet that she's in that one." I told him. His face looked at me in awe, and he blinked twice.

"Did you say that the sand told you?" He shook his head, "Never mind that. I've got to find her and find a way out. And it seems that I now have another person to break out of prison." He laughed as he shook his head.

"You're a troublemaker, Sahara. You'll owe me a kiss when I get you out." Kai winked at me and ran down the hallway.

I smiled and leaned back onto the sand, enjoying the feeling against my skin, as I waited to see who would come first - my killer or my captors.

I was lying back in the sand, waiting, and listening. I must have dozed off in the silence.

I was dreaming of the sand, and it was swallowing me. I sank below the sand's surface and opened my eyes. My vision was dark, and red. I waved my arm and felt the sand move with it. My arms were free. I kicked one leg out and the sand had fully embraced it, but it was separate from the other. I wasn't tied up. I tried to move my head and figure out where I was. The sand felt grainy against my face. My eyes were trying to comprehend what they were seeing; or rather what they weren't seeing.

Where was my cell? My jellyfished door? I couldn't see anything, so I listened. I could hear footsteps, but they were far away. I could hear my heartbeat in my chest, thumping in my heart. I could feel the presence of people a short distance away. In the cell next door, the person was pacing. The sand whispered my name. *Sahara.*

I stopped and listened hard, trying to figure out where it was coming from.

Sahara, you need to surface. And then I felt the push of the sand and my vision changed from red to yellow. The sand cleared from my face, and I was sitting on the floor of the cell.

I looked down at my hands and legs, the red scales fading into my tan skin. The kelp ties were gone. *I can swim in sand.* The thought echoed in my skull. *I can swim. In. The. Sand.*

I put my feet flat on the sand and felt the pulse of the ground. I could feel where people were disturbing the sand. I could feel that someone was coming down the hallway - wait no. Two people. They were walking, but they seemed to be moving fast. I sat against the far wall of my cell which was made of sand bricks. I felt the scales on my back transform on my skin, and then the wall felt cool and flowing, like water on my back. I leaned forward and watched as two guards stomped down the hall, checking the rooms as they passed.

The sand had told me to surface. It was sentient. Wait, is this what people meant about the sea giving them a choice? The sea could talk to them, give them missions, and give them a choice. I was never given a choice.

I saw someone run by and heard a guard shout, "Intruder!"

The flash of blue shorts made me smile as Kai was racing back out, the guards chasing him. "You were right! She is down there!" and he kept running, the guards following behind him.

I guess my killer was not going to rescue me, so I would have to face my captor.

Leaning back, I decided to see just how much control I had of my body while surrounded by the sand. At least I have the time for this now. I looked down at my legs and focused on the sand beneath them. I wanted my legs to sink into the sand. My skin slowly changed from skin to scale, and then they were floating on the sand. It felt weightless. I pushed down, and my legs plunged down into the cool sand below. It moved around me, allowing me to swing my legs freely like they were in water. The resistance was there, but not what I was expecting. My back was already scaled, and I decided to see if I could fall through the cell walls.

I lifted my legs out of the puddle of sand and stood against the wall and pushed. My hands changed and they slowly sank into the solid bricks. This was awesome. I kept pushing and pushing, and then summoned my courage and forced my face into the wall. The sand gave way easily, and I was all inside the sand. I lifted my leg and it moved with no resistance. I pushed through to the other side of the cell wall, and then I was falling. I landed with a thud on the floor of the cell next to mine, with sand solidifying behind me.

Yes! I thought, this is awesome! I can swim through sand. Now I stopped and listened to the sand as it rippled in front of my eyes like water. I was in full siren scales, my vision clicked into place with the yellow eyes. The cell next to me was empty, and there were no jellyfish stretched across the door. I leaned my head out and placed my hands on the sand bricks, feeling for footprints. There was no movement nearby, and the next cell was empty too. There was someone down a few cells. I walked down the hall, my hands always on the wall, feeling the pulse of movement in the sand.

I passed the empty cells and peered into the occupied one. The octopus-man was lying curled into a ball on the floor. A red jellyfish was stretched across the doorway, blocking my way in or out.

He glanced at me, and then bared his teeth, growling "Stay away from me. All the mermaids are going to be eaten by the sharks." He sneered.

"Octavius, is it?" I asked. My voice kind of echoed, but there was still no movement. He looked up at me. "I think you were very brave standing up to that bitch like that. That's why I got thrown in here too." I smiled at him.

"Wait, what? You're not in a cell?" He looked confused, "what could a mermaid do to get thrown into a sand cell?" he asked.

"I freed the Sirens."

"You what?! How- wait- what?" He stammered incoherently. "They will kill us all."

"The sirens don't want to kill anyone. We were forced to do what she asked, just like everyone else seems to be around here. Do you know how to remove the Jellyfish? I will let you out." I asked him.

The Jellyfish was the one who responded. "All you need to do is ask. I will move. I don't want to be here either" and then he proceeded to jiggle his stretched out tentacles.

"Oh! Mr. Jellyfish, would you please let me pass?" I asked him. Octavius gave me a weird look, but the red jellyfish brightened up. "Oh! Finally, a polite one! We hate this job. It's demeaning and demoralizing, and to have people walk through us feels awful. It hurts us as much as it hurts you." He released his tentacles from the doorway and sank to the floor. He looked up and asked, "Can you carry me to the water down the wall, there's a basin that they dunk us in, so we don't die.""Do you want to go back in the basin, or into the ocean?" I asked. His form perked up and he seemed to grow with excitement.

"You would take me to the ocean? For real? I would hug you if it wouldn't hurt!" He formed two of his tentacles into a heart shape. "Oh, Miss, they keep the shifter's skins in a closet up that way," He pointed to where I had come from.

"Thank you! Can I pick you up somehow?" I asked. Octavius was watching the exchange with a confused expression.

"They can speak?" He asked. "You can understand them?"

"Of course, they can speak, they are creatures of the sea." "No, no, no. Jellyfish aren't sentient, they're just angry balloons."

"The hell we are" The jellyfish spat out. "Stupid shifters can't understand us, but the fish do."

"Oh. I see. So, shifters can't understand you, but I somehow can. What else is wrong with me?" I asked out loud.

"You can pick me up where my head is. Carry me upside down, I'll flow my tentacles out around your hand. Just promise you won't throw me?" I laughed at the notion, then scooped him up, careful to avoid his long red tentacles. I told Octavius that his skin was being held in a closet down the hall. He thanked me and ran out.

I continued down the hallway, my new jellyfish friend held precariously in my arms.

"Who are you that you're so special to be able to talk to us lowly jellyfish?" He asked me.

"I don't know."

"You don't know who you are, or you don't know why? He asked back.

I thought about it as I continued down the hall. The air was damper, and I could hear the water lapping at the sand now. The jellyfish shook with anticipation, feeling like jello in my hands.

"I am Sahara, I am a siren, but not a siren. Apparently, I might be some sort of prophesied saviour. I don't know about that. There is a lady down here who might have some answers. That's why I'm going this way, and not running."

"Ah. My name is Jerry, by the way, and thank you for asking and being so kind."

"Nice to meet you, Jerry." Jerry the jellyfish. How cute. I reached the end of the hallway and turned right. There was a cell of sand blocks, but the bottom of the room was flooded. Another red jellyfish stretched across the door. I willed my legs to stay separate and placed Jerry into the water below.

"There you go, Jerry, I hope you can find some freedom too. Does the jellyfish on this door have a name?"

"That's Jonah. He's been holding that cell for years." He waved at me and bobbed down into the water.

I looked past Jonah and into the cell that was keeping a woman. Her dark orange-brown tail was dipped into the water, and her hands were tied above her head, holding her to the sand wall. Her long red hair was a perfect match for mine, and her eyes widened when she saw me.

"Excuse me, Mr. Jonah?" I tentatively asked the jellyfish. "Are you able to let me through please?"

"Wow, such manners from a mermaid. Who do you think you are?" he asked gruffly.

"I'm sorry, I'm not a mermaid. Could I place you into the ocean water over there for some time to relax?" I asked him.

"Wait, you can actually hear me?"

"She's great! She let me into the sea over here!" Jerry called, "Come and join me, Jonah!"

"Oh, alright." He released his grips and dropped into my hand, careful not to touch me. The woman in the cell stared in awe.

I placed Jonah beside Jerry in the pool of water, and he stretched and bobbed his head.

"Thank you, miss. I hope you find whatever it is you are looking for" Jerry said.

Then I walked into the cell and looked into a face that looked just like mine.

My mother.

I walked to the sand and sunk my hand into it and forced the ties up and out to release her. Her arms dropped like lead, and she slumped. I tried to pick her up, but she lifted herself and leaned against the solid wall. She looked at me and a small guttural sound came from her throat, "Sahara?" She asked. I nodded, and tears filled both our eyes.

"Are you Shannon? Or Brooke? Or both?" I asked her back, and she just nodded. She lifted her hands and started to sign.

"Sahara, my baby, you're all grown up! You are beautiful. But why are you here? In the cells? In the water?" Her eyes bulged as it fully dawned on her that I was here. "You are a siren?" she asked.

I reached down and offered my hand. "Can I carry you to the water so you can have a quick swim?"

"How is it that you speak so normally above the water?" She signed, instead.

I sat down beside her, this woman who looked just like me.

"I didn't die. I wasn't drowned in the sea. I am a siren, but not." I signed.

"Are you my mother?" I asked her out loud.

"I am your mother." she said, and her voice echoed off the walls, carrying her voice for miles. She covered her mouth, and I rested my hand on the sand walls. I felt no additional movements, nothing. I shook my head.

"It's okay, no one heard you.

"How are you here?" She signed again anyway.

"It's a very long story. But we're going to leave. And you are coming with me."

She shook her head.

I can't leave. I can't walk on sand anymore. If I try to leave, I'll turn to dust. I only have a few more years of service to the sea left, and then I can be free. Plus, that young man said he was going to find a way to free me. They have found LaReigne."

"But what if you don't have to be out of the water?" I was trying to think of a way when I felt the sands shift. I heard a whisper. *It's time to go, Sahara. Take her and we will carry you both to the water.*

I signed to my mother. "The sands say it's time to go. Grab my hand and trust me. Okay?"

"Sands?" She signed, looking perplexed. I reached for her hand and pulled her up. I lifted her out of the water. She was so skinny, so frail that it was almost too easy. I walked out of her cell and raced toward the dry sand, and when I felt the sand shift beneath me, I let it take over.

My feet sunk into the sand, and I heard a small voice shout:

"Go for it, girls! Get out of here!" I laughed a little as Jerry was shouting encouragement our way. The sand created a current, and we were pulled forward together. Her eyes were open in surprise, as the sands moved us so quickly. Soon we arrived at the closet full of skins.

She tapped my shoulder and signed "Wait. Get the skins."

I opened the door and saw a pile of skins. Shark skins, seal skins, squid skins, whale skins. The octopus skins were missing, but I figured Octavius probably snatched them and ran. Brooke grabbed the skins and bundled them against us, and we were moving again.

I heard a shout and felt the movement of feet in the hallway to our left, and we went around the right corner. We were headed straight for the ballroom we had left, but then we turned into an unseen crevice in the walls.

There was a pool of water, and two seals that just hopped out of it with wide eyes. I quickly put Brooke into the water and tossed the skins in after her. She dived down and turned into a fully orange-brown siren.

"Lass, you broke out of jail all on your own?" Lachlan asked, bewilderment in his voice, as he nudged me with his cute seal nose, whiskers twitching.

"Sort of" I replied.

"Stay up here," Aerwyna said. "Don't go through those tunnels just yet. They're going to discover that you are missing soon." "Especially because Kai was about to lead Phillip and the dolphins into a charge to free the jails." Lachlan said, and he looked me over.

"Are you hurt at all? Did they do anything to you?"

"I'm fine." I told him, crossing my arms.

"What do you mean you are fine. You are a crazy woman! Challenging Queen Loralei like that. I thought we would be coming to pick up a corpse!" His face said it all. He was scared for me.

I reached out and touched him, the blubbery seal a smooth sensation against my skin.

"I'm sorry for scaring you. But I couldn't let another person die, and I couldn't let another siren be used anymore."

Brooke nodded underwater, and then lifted her head. She used the same guttural throat sound so as not to echo in the chamber.

"Lachlan and Aerwyna? The children of Alistair?" She asked. They nodded, and I blanched. She was his sister. I'm so dumb, I thought as I looked at the two of them.

"Thank you for always being on our side." she whispered and dipped into the water again.

"Always, Miss." Aerwyna said. "You saved our father from the tyrant once, but now we need to ask your favour again."

"First, let's all get out of the palace, and out of Aquacity. This isn't going to be easy," Lachlan said.

There was a knock at the crevice, and Philip strode in wearing nothing, his skin hooked around his neck like a cape. He looked at me, surrounded by the seals and Brooke in the pool, as Brooke threw out two skins from the water, one Seal skin and one dolphin skin.

Lachlan's wide eyes rounded and got even bigger.

"She can't wear a seal skin. They will know."

"They won't know." Phillip said. "Kai and his crazy antics are the distraction. The sirens are already fleeing Aquacity. Ashera is going with them. They are fleeing all the way to the octopi's territory, on Octavius's orders. Turtleback Beach is where I am going to meet them. Namiko and Kai will meet up after." He paused and looked at me, smiling.

"I think after this little charade and show today, we will have many more who seek us out. Thanks to you, Sahara."

"But how do we get out?" I asked the dolphin, trying very hard not to look anywhere except his face.

"Brooke is going to put on the dolphin skin and come with us. Lachlan and Aerwyna, take Sahara and meet us there. It's going to be a long swim. At least in a seal skin, she will be able to go onto land. Since Brooke can't go on land, it would be best that she's a dolphin."

Lachlan still shook his head, his mouth opened and closed, but he had no argument for the Dolphin Ambassador.

"Aerwyna, help her into the sealskin. Phillip, take good care of Brooke, please. We will meet you at Turtleback Beach." There was a noise in the hallway, and Phillip slipped out. I could see Ian out there, and after a few words, he nodded solemnly and took off down the hallway.

"Ian and Kai will create the distractions we need." I picked up the skin and handed it to Brooke.

"Hello, Miss Brooke, long time no see. Do you need help getting into the dolphin skin, or have you got it?"

"I got it" She signed. Then Phillip and Brooke both stepped into the skins and transformed. I blinked and she was a dolphin. She looked at me with her big eyes and I saw the message in them. *Be safe. See you soon.*

Aerwyna lifted her skin and stepped out of it. I had picked the other skin up from the floor and was holding it in my hands. She tossed it over my head, and it felt like she buttoned something, and zipped something and then I felt smaller, like I was being consumed by the skin. My vision changed again, and I felt heavy and fat.

I opened my eyes and saw that the room had changed, it appeared as a full greyscale, but with high contrast. My whiskers twitched. Wait. I could feel my whiskers? I had whiskers? I could also feel the vibrations in the air. Aerwyna was already back into her skin and hobbling towards the water.

"C'mon, Sahara, we've got to go. Iin and Kai are going to create a scene and point them in the other direction. It's a long swim" she said as she dived into the water.

I followed or tried to hobble over to the water tunnel in the room. It was clear instead of blue, and the sensations overwhelmed me.

"Aye, c'mon, Lass. Follow me", and then he head-butted me into the water. The water slid over my skin, and my whiskers felt all the motions. Even with my eyes closed, I could still see and feel the location of every nook and cranny.

"Is it always this overwhelming?" I asked, trying to make sense of all the new sensations. Aerwyna swam to the bottom and was collecting the other skins Brooke and I had nabbed from the closet. Phillip and Brooke had taken the rest of the skins.

"You get used to the sensations but try to focus on swimming. Use your body to give you momentum, and you just keep going. Flip your legs and tail up, and beat down." he explained, then he nudged me again.

"She could barely swim as a siren; I have no idea how she's going to do it now" Aerwyna muttered.

"She'll do great. She's a beautiful seal, aren't ya, Lass?"

"She's beautiful, yes, but she still can't swim worth a damn," and then she came up underneath me, and pushed.

The heave I got from Aerwyna sent me down the tunnel and the sensations were beyond overwhelming. I could feel in my face where everything was, how the current was moving. There was a group of merfolk up ahead and Lachlan swam around to my left side. I heard his bark, but the words were *Turn left,* and then he shoved me over to the left.

We turned down another tunnel as I flipped my new weight and hefty tail and tried to steer myself. I was slow, but Lachlan and Aerwyna stayed with me. We dodged several more groups of guards, and I could hear the shouts and commotion.

Lachlan barked again, *you need to look like you belong. We're going to be in the city soon.*

I didn't say anything and just focused on the swim. The tunnels and corals were all shades of black and grey, and the rock was marble. We were in the main part of the palace.

Lachlan slowed and made eye contact with Aerwyna. I could sense someone else nearby, but couldn't make heads or tails of who, or what was out there. Aerwyna swam out slowly, almost lazily and called out "Hey, did they find the prisoners? I think I heard them calling for help." A pair of guards stopped and shouted "Who are you? No one can leave the palace right now."

"I am Aerwyna, the Selkie Ambassador. I am alone, and my brother is out searching for the missing siren. Why are you not out searching?" She sounded so regal, so confident. I gently nudged into Lachlan, hoping he would still be by my side if anything happened to his sister. *I still can't believe I didn't realise that they were siblings sooner.* Lachlan nudged me back gently, but his eyes were glued to the corner where his sister had gone.

"We are required to stay here to block the exit." The guards announced.

"Well then, please escort me out of the palace so that I can find my brother." She demanded from them. The guards paused and I could sense that one even swallowed hard, before opening the door and leading Aerwyna outside. Does Lachlan want me to do that? I can't do that. My voice is so different. He nudged me, and pushed me along, toward the open door. I was terrified, but I kept going. We swam as swiftly as possible, and then made a break for it. Aerwyna was off to the left, making the guards escort her around, "looking" for Lachlan. She turned to look at us and shooed us onwards.

Lachlan and I turned to the right, and I swam as fast as I could for the city streets. He nudged me the whole way out of the city, and we passed the jellyfished door quickly.

I whispered a silent apology to the jellyfish as I swam through, my large form and blubbery body barely feeling the sting this time. There was a shout behind us, and Lachlan pushed me forward. I could hear the commotion of the city, as the merfolk got all stirred up for a chase. I shuddered but kept flapping my heavy tail.

Once we were out in the open ocean, Lachlan pushed me up, toward the surface. I understood the intention and pushed myself upwards.

I hadn't seen Aerwyna following, and I was feeling guilty. She should be here; she could be in danger; she could be caught. We breached the surface, my eyes marveling at the sight. The colours were different, the air was different, and I was overwhelmed by everything. So much had happened.

"Hey Lass, d'you think you can porpoise? It goes fast. If I explain it, do you think you can follow?" Lachlan asked, out of breath.

"Can I what?" I managed to spit out.

"Jump and swim," He explained it, and after several attempts, I was jumping, and swimming faster than I ever had before. He led the way, setting the pace, but ensured I was keeping up. Swimming for my life was something I never thought I would have to do, much less more than once.

We finally neared an island, and he said we should stop. I was exhausted, but I wasn't going to let him know. I was capable of this. I could push through it. I had to. I caused this mess. This was all my fault. We reached the beach. I managed to pull myself onto the shore, and then I collapsed. The weight was too much, the swimming, the running, the adrenaline, the guilt. I sobbed into the sand. Lachlan was out of his skin in no time and pulling me out of mine. Once I was freed from the blubbery suit and weight of the seal, Lachlan hugged me close to his chest.

"It's all right, Lass. We're okay. We will rest here, and we can continue our swim in the morning. We should be okay to hide here."

"But what about Aerwyna? And Phillip, And Kai, and Ian … and?" I asked as I sobbed into his chest.

"Shush," he said as he stroked my hair. "Aerwyna is fine. She will be fine. She's tough, that one. She will catch up to us, just as we will meet up with everyone else. You are in shock again, love."

His muscular body was pressed against mine, and he scooped me up and walked further onto the island. My eyes were tearing up, and the water was streaming down my cheeks, but I have no idea if it was my tears or the salt water from my hair. My brain wasn't working, and his chest was so warm, so very warm.

I awoke later in the night. His arm was wrapped around my waist, and he was snoring lightly as he cuddled up against my back. Something splashed in the water, and I shuddered and shook Lachlan awake.

"Something is in the water" I whispered. He nodded but said nothing. I rested my hands on the beach and reached out to the sands to listen. They could only tell me the little hermit crabs were below the surface of the sand, but not what was in the water. I could feel the entirety of the island, and everything touching the sand. It was small. We heard no other splashes, and I felt no movement on the isle. I leaned into Lachlan's arms and wrapped them tightly around me.

He nuzzled down toward my ear.

"You have nothing to fear, love. I will protect you. Get some more rest." I trusted this man. He had saved my life, more than a few times now. I smiled and settled into his arms. He gave me a gentle squeeze and soon his breathing was steady and shallow. I listened to his breathing, willing my heart to match his steady pace, and soon drifted off.

I woke up as dawn was just cresting over the water, and Lachlan was nowhere in sight. I felt for the sand on the island and found that he had left the island. He was gone. My heart sank into my stomach, as I cried again. He ran away and left me alone. I was too much trouble, and he left me. I was a nuisance. A pest. I'd ruined everything they were trying to work toward. I was nothing but a coward, who ran from danger. I sat down in the sand and tried to listen to the sea, but it was silent. The only sounds were the waves on the beach, so I made my way toward the shore. I picked up the discarded seal skin. I looked around but knew that Lachlan's was missing. I tied the skin around my waist like I'd seen Aerwyna do. This skin belonged to someone, and I wouldn't just leave it behind. If I'm going to return it, I would need to go to Turtle Beach Island. And I would get there on my own.

I didn't know the right direction to go, but I knew that I could understand the sea animals. So, I walked off the beach, and down into the water. I swam down into the dark waters, looking for something to talk to.

It wasn't too long before I found a school of rainbow-coloured fish.

"Excuse me, can you understand me?" I asked the school of fish darting about, cringing as my siren voice echoed.

"Sure, we can understand you. Do you understand us?" it sounded like the fish all answered in unison, and from every direction.

"Yes! Great! Do you know the way to Turtle Beach Island?" I asked them.

"Wait, you understand us?" They asked again and swarmed closer together.

"Yes, I understand you. Can you please tell me how to get to Turtle Beach Island?"

The school floundered a minute, and then they swam around me, trapping me into a mini vortex in the sea. I stayed still and let them be, and then asked more firmly,

"Are you able to help me at all?"

"You are a siren, but not a siren. You are of the sea, but not. You can understand us. You are different from the others." The chorus of sounds came from the school of fish.

"We can help her," then they stopped their vortex and made an arrow.

"Swim that way for about forty miles. You should stay near the surface, so you won't get lost. You will pass three small islands, and when the tide is low, they form one big island. Turtle Beach is about ten miles beyond that. If you can understand us, ask the schools near the islands for help."

"Thank you so much! I appreciate it. Do you have names?"

"Names? Names? Names?" came a chorus of questions, echoing in the water.

"We are Iris."

"Thank you, Iris." I listened to the school and began my solo journey. Swimming in what I thought was an easterly direction. I got close to the surface and managed to porpoise as a siren, which was exciting since I was moving quickly, and I could watch for the islands the school mentioned.

I continued until the sun was high in the sky before I heard something swimming fast behind me. I tried to outswim it, but to no avail. It gained on me until it was right behind me. It knocked into me and I screamed.

"Lass, calm down! It's me." I stopped swimming and stared at the grey seal who had caught up to me.

"What the bloody hell do you think you are doing, swimming out in open water by yourself?! Damn it, Sahara, you could have been lost, or captured. Or drowned or dust..."

"Where was I? Where were you?" I yelled back. "I wake up at the crack of dawn, and you're gone. Your skin is gone, and there's nothing. Not a damn trace of you. I thought you left me for dead." I was crying this time, the hot tears streaking down my face. "You left me..." I whispered, but he just nudged against me and tucked his head against mine. His whiskers tickled my face, and his eyes held mine.

"Sahara, I said I would protect you and I mean that. You are worth protecting. I didn't leave you, and I don't intend to leave you. I went to get you some food, and to send a message to Aerwyna. When I came back to the isle, you were gone. I thought that maybe the merfolk got you. Taken you. Killed you." His voice wavered as he leaned against me. "The creatures around here aren't my usual branch of contacts, but they will get the message to her." He swam ahead, "Come on, love, it's still a long swim, and I bet you haven't eaten in a great while. There should be an island ahead with some fruits for you, unless you want raw fish, from that school there." If he had an eyebrow, it would have been raised, and I giggled.

We swam in sync for a while, a siren and selkie, jumping through the waters. The island was plentiful, and I had a few fruits before we were on our way.

We were quiet, forcing ourselves along, and then Lachlan stopped.

"Shush, Lass. Sharks ahead. Can you wear the seal skin again?" He asked.

"I can't put it on myself." I told him, shaking my head. We sank below the water, and I saw the large island ahead. The sharks in the water were swimming in a group of three.

"Can you believe they released the sirens? Now, how are we going to get human meat?"

"It's about time someone stood up to that tyrant queen"

"Yeah, I hope she brings better things to the sea.""I'm going to miss chaos, but that was one smart siren.""Sir en-thing, she had legs on land."

"Do you think she'll make it out here?"

I smiled, listening to their gossip. They weren't upset or searching for me.

"Lachlan, I don't think they're against us." I whispered.

I slowly swam up toward them, "Excuse me?" I called out, and three sharks spun and stared at me. The one on the left dropped his jaw.

"It's you!" "The siren thing!"

"The saviour!"

"Are you here to kill us?"

"Um, I don't think so. We're trying to escape right now" I said

"Who's the seal?" the middle shark asked.

"My companion. He's showing me the way. I don't suppose you are able to help us?" I asked, raising my eyebrow hopefully. Lachlan was tugging at my arm.

They gave me a blank stare, then a wicked smile crossed their faces. "Oh, we can help." Except it didn't sound helpful at all, and they charged.

"Shit. Sahara, Swim! Swim for your life." Lachlan called, swimming away.

"Oh! The ambassador is with you."

"Mmm. Tasty seal meat" and they sped off towards him. I swam as fast I could, and saw the tri-island grouping ahead. "Lachlan, get to the islands." I yelled. I swam like hell for them, dodging their snapping jaws. They were on my tail, and I jumped out of water, and hit the shore. When I reached the beach, I pulled Lachlan up to safety. He quickly shed his skin and started to run inland. I planted my legs into the sandy dune. I focused on the sand and water, and when the sharks came barreling up the beach, I solidified them in the sand, creating bricks like the cells that I had been in. I smiled triumphantly, as the sharks were trapped, and unable to get free.

"I'm so sorry, I know sharks need to keep swimming to survive. I will release you if you promise not to chase us."

"Wait, did she really say she would release us?" They were flopping about in the puddle of water, but unable to move.

"Are you as crazy as the Blue Queen?"

"Will you keep your word?" The third one asked.

"I mean it. I don't want to kill anyone. I just want to figure out who I am, and what is going on."

"You aren't going to force us to listen to a siren's call?"
"Or shred us?"

"Or have us watch our brothers and sisters be forced to do her bidding?"

"What? No, I just want to figure out who I am and how I can help." I released the sand, and the sharks were released back into the water, and were swimming again, and relief flooded their faces.

"The only thing I ask of you, is that you let me get away," I told them.

"We didn't see you." "You haven't been this way" Take out the tyrant, would you? So, we can have our family back?" The last shark gave me a look, and I smiled. "I will do my best, for everyone."

I ran over to Lachlan, who was coughing and doubled over in the sand, clutching his leg.

"Shit, they bit you, didn't they?" I saw the blood seeping from his leg into the sand. I looked around, and found nothing, so I tore a strip off my white dress and wrapped it around his leg. It turned crimson quickly, but the makeshift tourniquet was working. We're only about ten miles away," Lachlan said, looking out over the horizon, "If we get to Turtle Beach, they have healers there." He tried to get up, and I stopped him.

"You're hurt. We can wait here for a bit. Make sure this has stopped bleeding. I don't want you getting an infection." I told him, and he sat back onto the sand.

"How did you do that, with the sand?" He asked me as I tended his leg. I ripped another piece of the wet cloth from my dress and wrapped his leg more firmly, creating a bandage.

"I'm not sure exactly when I realised I had an affinity with the sand. But it kept calling to me, sending me dreams. I can swim in the sand. And it talks to me. You know how your whiskers can feel all the sensations in the water, all the little movements of the air and currents? Well, if I concentrate, I can feel and *see* and sense what is going on with the sand. I can sink into it, and it will form a liquid-like substance, or be solid." He looked up at me and winced as I tied the material tight.

"You are incredible. The most amazing person I've ever met," He smiled and leaned forward, grabbing my hands. His hands were calloused, and mine were smooth, and he squeezed them tight.

"I am in awe of you, Sahara. You had my attention, right from the get-go. But I think there might be more to you than meets the eye." He pulled his long hair from his bun and let it down. The waves fell around his face and framed it. Damn. He was beautiful.

"Are you delirious?" I asked, feeling his forehead.

"Not delirious, but I did almost get eaten by a shark. That makes a man think, okay?" His smile was warm, and I could sense the longing from him.

I was looking into his eyes, and they searched mine, looking to see if it was okay. I leaned forward, just a little bit, and closed my eyes as his lips captured mine. The salty taste of the water on his lips met with mine, and we revelled in the moment.

The sound of the water around us stopped as my heart beat new rhythms in my chest. His hands found the back of my neck and the kiss deepened. I was lost to this man, who would protect me from sharks and to all the bad things in his world.

When we parted, we were breathing heavily. His forehead pressed against mine, our hair tangled together. He untangled it, and then tied my hair back into a ponytail with his tie.

"We need to keep going, Sahara, it's only about ten miles now. Once we reach Turtle Beach, we will be safe from the tyrant queen for a while." He rose and picked up his skin but held tight to my hand.

"I won't let any harm come to you, love." He smiled and slid his skin over his body and was once again the cute seal that was as large as any man. His whiskers twitched, and he hobbled towards the water. I stuck my hands into the sand and helped him along, making it so that the sands were carrying him.

"This is such a strange sensation." "You're telling me." I put my hands to my lips, remembering the warmth, and saltiness of his lips, the tickle of his beard, and my heart did a flip. I ran and dove into the water, changing into the siren form and we headed out for the last stretch.

The last stretch was long and arduous, but uneventful. We could see the island, but Lachlan was breathing hard, and he was concentrating intently in order to make it. I noticed the trail of red he was leaving in the water and realised he was still bleeding. I swam up beside him, tugged him the last of the way, and dragged him onto the shore. We both collapsed with the effort.

I heard a shout, and Phillip and Kai were running toward us. They picked us both up and started to bring us out of the water. "Is Aerwyna here yet?" Lachlan asked, his voice hoarse.

"He's hurt, a shark bit his leg. Help him first." I called to the boys, as I let the sand surround me and give me relief.

Phillip stuck his fingers together and issued a shrill whistle. Ian and Ashj came running, followed by a couple of others I didn't recognise.

There was a lot of commotion, and suddenly I was being carried

away, by a set of strong arms. I looked up to see Kai's brown eyes and tattoos on his chest, his hair loose around his broad shoulders. Funny, he and Lachlan were similar in appearance, except for the shade of their skin, and facial hair.

'Is Lachlan okay?" I asked him, trying to look for Lachlan.

"He's going to be okay. The dolphins are getting him cleaned up, and they will fix his leg. We need to get you looked over. You've made a hell of a mess, Troublemaker." He was smiling.

"What about Aerwyna, has she made it?" I asked.

"She hasn't reached the island yet. She is a very strong and smart girl. She will make it. I have full confidence in that one." I closed my eyes as he carried me, trying to catch my breath.

"Is Brooke okay?" I asked suddenly, startling Kai and he almost dropped me.

"God, Sahara," He laughed. "She's here, I'm taking you to her, and the other fugitive sirens and merfolk. We need to get you cleaned up and checked over too." He then hoisted me over his shoulder. "You're such a troublemaker. Freeing the Sirens on a whim." He was shaking his head, but I could feel the laughter in his chest. He carried me to a shelter, similar to the one Echo Island, but much larger. He knocked on the screen door, then opened it.

"Ladies! I'm coming in. And bringing a very important guest." He walked through and placed me on a giant moss ball that was partially submerged in water. The room on the beach had a pool of water in the center. It wasn't overly large, and it was occupied. Brooke sat on the edge with her tail in the water. Cordelia and Constance were also in the pool. Cordelia was brushing Constance's hair and when Kai set me down, he winked.

"At least I got to somewhat rescue you. Even if it was just from the beach to here. Don't start talking until I leave the room! I don't have the earplugs in!" he warned the others, and they nodded. "I'll tell everyone to wear them."

"Tell me when Aerwyna makes it, and when Lachlan's okay? Please?" I called to him as he was leaving.

"Sure thing, Troublemaker." He closed the door, leaving me with Brooke, Cordelia and Constance.

"Sahara." Brooke spoke my name. The sound that resonated from her throat was high and melodic, like a whisper and a shout all at once. I shook my head, and she swam towards me.

"Are you my Sahara?" She asked quietly, but it felt familiar.

"I think so. My father's name is Roger." Her face lit up and tears started to stream down her face.

"Is he okay? I was dragged from him so many years ago. I'm so sorry, Sahara. I wanted to see you grow up. I ... I ..." She trailed off and I hopped into the water and hugged her, tears forming in my own eyes.

"He's okay. Still as deaf and as stubborn as ever. I don't know if he knows where I am. Or whether I am alive or not." I cried into my mother's arms.

"Hush now, Sahara, don't cry. That man will sail the seven seas to find you. He was supposed to keep you safe from the water, not allowing you into this mess. I even tried to make sure you knew as a child. I could only whisper the words, not sing them, but I think I can sing them now."

Hush little baby, don't you cry, I will sing you a lullaby, Dream *of things that are dry as sand,*
Keep your feet forever on land.

I joined her in singing, remembering the song, and how I sang it on stage, It was a lost memory from my childhood.

Hush little baby, remember me,
There are dangers lurking in the sea.
When the moon is high and the tide is strong,
Stay away and remember my song.
Close your eyes and get some sleep,
And in my heart you'll forever be.

My mother hugged me close, the tears streaming down her face.

Cordelia and Constance were watching, holding each other and Cordelia had tears in her eyes.

"Are you mother and daughter?" I asked. Cordelia nodded. "Thank you, Sahara. I owe you a great debt for what you did for us at the palace. You saved her life."

"No, anyone who had the power to stop her, should."

"This is what I was afraid of," Brooke said. "You are the prophesied one."

"Okay, what is this prophecy? It's not the first I've heard of it. Phillip told me something about it." And then as if on cue, there was a knock at the door.

"Excuse me, Ladies. Can we come in? It's Kai, Phillip and Lachlan." I swear my heart flipped when I heard Lachlan's name. I was so worried about him and his leg.

"Come in," I called, knowing my voice wouldn't hurt them. The three of them entered the room, and I noticed Lachlan was limping on his left leg. He was helped over to the Moss Ball to sit beside Phillip. They had found clothes to cover themselves, but only shorts.

"Brooke," Phillip said. "We have earplugs in, so we should be able to hear your voices, and not jump into the water. But if we jump, please don't drown us." He laughed, and Constance smiled, the bandages on her chin and throat not stopping the smile.

"I promise to not let any of you drown," Brooke said.

"Good, now, will you tell us the prophecy that we are doomed to see fulfilled."

Brooke took a deep breath and began to recite it, holding my hand tightly.

Born of land and born of sea
Sing the scales in harmony
When tide is low and moon is strong
She sings aloud a siren song
Sung amidst the symphony
The vocal choir is the key.
A resonance of sea and land
Force the fiends to show their hand
Dissonance, discord it brings
Tones in key she still must sing
A show of brand-new melody
United ends the tyranny.

When she stopped the room was silent, as we digested the prophecy.

"I hadn't heard it whole before" Lachlan broke the silence.

"Nor have I. But born of land and born of sea is definitely the hybrid of siren that Sahara is." Phillip said. "She is the first siren to be born, and not made by the sea."

"But what about the vocal choir?" asked Kai. "And it gets quite dark, dissonance and discord, fiends, and tyranny?"

"That's a lot to process," I said. And I hopped out of the water, letting my legs dry and split.

"Sounds like we're facing a battle between sea and land." Constance signed.

"No, I don't think sea and land is the fight, I think they need to work together to bring unity." Phillip again. "But Sahara and her voice will be the key. She will bring peace to the oceans."

I let them process and try to twist and spin it to what they wanted, but I left the room and closed the door. I walked along the shoreline and heard my name being called. I looked back but didn't stop. I started running along the beach, and let the sands carry me along.

I reached the far side of the beach, with my head still reeling. What would I have to do to defeat her? Would I have to fight her? Kill her? I don't want to kill anyone. I am a human. I have a voice, but this isn't what it's for. A voice is for speaking and singing, and bringing people together, not dissonance and discord.I heard a small splash in the water, and a seal popped her head up. It was Aerwyna, but she wasn't swimming, just floating.

I ran out and pulled her onto shore, using the sands to help carry her.

"Aerwyna, oh my god. Are you okay?" I tried to hear her heart and felt her skin for the seal to let her out. She had a knife sticking out of her back, and it was dripping blood into the water. I finally found the release and pulled her skin back. She was pale, and barely breathing. I left the knife in, and put pressure on it, and cried for help, yelling and shouting. And then I called the sands, and sunk into the sand, using my hands to carry her, and swam in the sand, bringing her the way I came, shouting the whole way. "HELP. HELP ME." I was crying now and Aerwyna was barely breathing. I finally heard a shout as I neared the shore, and Ian, Aishj and Ashera ran toward me. I was sobbing, trying to explain that there was a knife in her back.

Ashera paled when she saw the knife. "That's a royal guard's knife" she said quietly. "She was stabbed close to here."

The two dolphins whisked her away, and Ashera knelt in the sand and hugged me.

"I am so sorry, Sahara. I never meant any harm to any of you. But how the hell are you waist-deep in the sand and moving in it?" "I can swim in the sand," I replied simply, trying to dry my eyes. "Oh, my gods, please go tell Lachlan."

"Tell me what?" He asked, as he hobbled down the beach. He nodded to Ashera. "Tell me what?" He asked more desperately as he looked between us.

"Sahara found Aerwyna" Ashera started, "But she's very badly injured, she was ... she was stabbed with a royal guard's knife"

His eyes grew large and he balled his hands into fists. "That fucking

bitch better hope to God that Aerwyna lives. If my nephew doesn't have a mother because of her, I swear to the sea I will slit her fucking throat myself." He growled, full of rage and hate. His eyes were dark, and he stood there shaking. I lifted myself to my feet, and Ashera gave me her arm. "Ian and Aisjh took her to the octopi healers. I hope she'll be okay. Sahara carried her all the way from the other side of the beach here." She said and pointed in the direction the dolphins took her. Lachlan tried to run after Aerwyna, his bad leg hindering him. I let him go, Ashera following behind him, telling him the way.

Why is there so much hate and division in the sea? How could I possibly be the key for repairing all this? I sank onto my knees and stared at the ocean. How was I ever going to bring peace to all the different factions, groups and everything. This was too much to put onto one person. A person who didn't even know all of this existed a week ago.

A week. I've only been out here a week, and I've already stirred up so much drama. I had to kill sailors and sink a ship. I learned of a prophecy, and that I was now apparently the key to the prophecy. I refused an order from the queen, showed off, and freed the sirens. I got sent to jail, and broke out, breaking out the Octopus Ambassador, and my own mother, who I had believed to be dead for the last twenty years. I fled from the queen and her guard, and two selkies were hurt because I failed at swimming.

They don't deserve a saviour who can't help them. I am not that person.

"It's not me." I whispered.

"What's not you?" came a reply. Namiko was walking towards me. The sands hadn't given me any indication that she was there, I must have been too unfocused.

"I'm not the prophesied one. I can't be. There's too much to do. It's too much." She sat beside me in the sands and looked out of the sea.

"Maybe it's not you, yet." She said simply.

"Yet?" I asked, looking at her.

"A prophecy is all ambiguous and strange. It doesn't say exactly who, or exactly when, just that something will happen. It will happen when it happens." She smiled at me.

"Maybe it's just not yet."

"But things are so bad already, there's so much fighting, killing, and torture." "And blackmail and division and separation." Namiko finished. "Those are the things that precede a war. There are two sides, and both sides think they are doing the right thing. I don't want the fighting. No one does, but we aren't going to let them steamroll us either, so to bring balance to the ocean, we will have to fight." She hugged her knees to her chest. "I just hope that those held captive, and those who give their lives are fighting for themselves and their loved ones, and not just following blindly." Tears were on her face. "My parents died in an accident many years ago. It's just my sister and I, and they took her from me. To make me obedient, they took her on land, and made her learn to sing. If she didn't cooperate, or If I didn't, they threatened to kill us. If I'm going to die either way, I'm going to fight for it."

I felt the footsteps this time, and someone was behind us. "They took my parents." Kai said, sitting on the other side of me. "I have no idea where they are, but they aren't at the manor on the isle, where Nam's sister is. Nor are they anywhere in Aquacity. The palace is huge, and I've searched every inch. If you noticed, the cells are mostly empty. They keep their prisoners outside the city and hold us hostage by separation. Do this, or you'll never see the person you love again. 'Peacekeeping' they call it." Kai shook his head. "All it has done is breed hate and anger. This is a long time coming. We need to remove Loralei from power."

"And then what?" I asked. "After she is removed from power, there's a power vacancy. Who takes control? Who leads the way? Who ushers in the era of peace? Because it's not me."

"You're right. We used to be a free society, with no monarchy. We were governed by the people. The queen is new, and she is a totalitarian, she wants full control of the ocean, but-" She paused and looked at Kai.

"Loralei wasn't always this way. She went to shore one day with Melody and they visited Araxie's manor. They were both different when they returned that day."

"Different? How?" I asked, concerned.

"They were angrier and pushier. They commanded and demanded." Kai said.

"They became hateful and full of spite, lashing out and saying they were going to change the sea. Something changed them in the manor. And I worry about my sister, that she too will be like them." "Your little sister is too sweet for that, Nam." I heard a splash in the water, and immediately rose to my feet. So did Kai and Namiko.

Then four heads popped out of the water, changing from siren to human. Nixie, Pasha, Raidne and Maya all looked on.

"Sahara" Maya called, and the sound forced Kai and Namiko to cover their ears. She put a hand over her mouth and covered it. "Sorry" she signed.

"How did you get here?" I asked them.

"Aerweyna told us where you were going."

"We got lost along the way, but we eventually made it!"

Kai put his fingers together and whistled, and soon some shifters I didn't recognise came down the beach.

Kai started issuing directions. "Get some towels in water and bring them here. We've got to get them to the pool in the middle of the island. It's the only safe spot for them right now."

They moved quickly and then there were a chain of people helping the sirens move from the sea into the pool. I followed them into the room which had been expanded by moving the screens.

"Sorry for the surprise, and lack of room, Ladies. We weren't expecting so many sirens. We have issued earplugs to everyone, but still, this could be dangerous for us."

"Wait. I think I can make the pool larger." I sunk my feet into the sand, and guided the sand, shifting and making the pool larger and deeper. The water was coming from beneath, and it trickled in, filling the pool. There was now enough room for all the sirens to fit comfortably in the middle of this island.

"Kind of feels like we're back on Donut Island, doesn't it?" Raidne signed.

"Except we are surrounded by people who will help us, not try to hurt us?" Pasha responded. They all nodded in agreement. Maya hugged Constance and they went under the water. I looked around at the people in the room. On this island. I am surrounded by people who want my help. People who need my help, who need me. Refugees. We are all important to someone, and we all need to help each other.

Maybe Namiko was right. I wasn't ready, yet. Yet. But that meant I could be ready. I would be ready, and this was just the beginning of the story. I would do what I could to fight for these people, their home, their way of life and their loved ones. And maybe, just maybe, sometime soon, I would be ready to fulfil the prophecy.

T he island was buzzing with activity. There were so many refugees, merfolk, shifters, and creatures alike. The sirens were practicing a new song I had taught them, one of the ones I had composed for my choir. It was beautiful, their voices making it sound so much more ethereal than my choir ever did. The flute wasn't even needed.As I was wandering, I found a pool of jellyfish on the island.

"Red Siren!" they cried. "You saved Jerry and Jonah, so we've come to help. We have lots of jellyfish here." I smiled and stopped and chatted with them.

"You guys are wonderful. Thank you for your assistance."

"We can be wielded as weapons. Throw us at them, and we'll sting them until they are paralyzed." I blinked a couple times, before laughing. The claim reassured me about their intent, and I called over to Octavius. He, too. had thanked me profusely for freeing him from his prison cell in the Aquacity Palace.

"Octavius, these jellyfish want to help. They offered to be thrown and sting any who aren't with us."

"It still amazes me that you can speak with the animals as well as the shifters." He looked into the pool of jellyfish, and waved a hand at them, his tentacled skin tied around his waist like a belt. "Thank you kindly. We will take all the help we can get."

I wandered off in search of the rest of the Octopi shifters and came across another hut nearby. I heard the hint of a Scottish accent and knocked on the door. "Lachlan?" I asked tentatively.

"Aye, Lass, come in."

He looked so disheveled, his long hair hanging loosely across his shoulders, and his whiskers looked limp and sad. Aerwyna was laying on a cot in the room. She hadn't awakened yet, but she was alive. Barely. I reached over and took hers and Lachlan's hands. His sad brown eyes looked into mine. "I'm sorry, Lachlan. I know she's your sister, and you need to take care of her, but you need to take care of you, too.

"Please go take a rest. I will stay here with her. Go get your leg bandage changed for a clean one."

"I'm fine." he huffed as he rose from his seat. He teetered unsteadily.

"You're not fine." I said as he leaned into me. "I promise, if anything changes, I will come and get you. Go rest."

"You promise me?" His eyes were full of pain. "I can't lose her."

I leaned in and hugged him tightly. "I promise to protect her, Lachlan. Like you've protected me." He rested his forehead against mine and sagged, his weight pulling against mine. "Go get some rest. She needs you to be healthy too." He finally nodded and left the room, calling for the octopus healer as the door closed.

I sat with Aerwyna, watching her, and her shallow breaths. The knife had missed her spine, thank god, but she was still gravely injured. I saw her sealskin on the foot of the bed, so I dug through the baskets in the corner. I found a needle and some red thread. *It will have to do,* I thought, and I sewed the hole closed on the back of her skin. Then I covered her with it, on top of the blanket that was on the cot. She stirred and coughed, and her eyes fluttered.

"Sahara?" She whispered hoarsely. I reached over and grabbed the glass of water and handed it to her.

"Yes, I'm here. I'll call for Lachlan." I said, getting up.

"No - wait..." I stopped and turned around, looking at her. "I need you to live, and he needs to be here" I said.

"I have something I need to tell you first," she said, grabbing my hand. "I'm not dying, I promise. Just like you promised Lachlan that you would protect me." She winked. My eyes widened, and I looked back at her. "I heard it all. He really cares about you," she squeezed my hand, and I could feel it in my heart.

"But and it hurts me to say this. I like you. And I like you and him. I do. But you can't be with him." She squeezed my hand.

"What- why?" I asked her, perplexed.

"You are dangerous; part siren, part human, and from what the rumours say, you are destined to bring peace to the ocean. We've both been injured in this twisted quest, and I can't have him giving his life for you," she said, with tears in her eyes. "I have a son, and husband, trapped on shore. Their skins were part of those that you rescued from the palace. I carried them here, but they slowed me down. The royal guards caught up with me. I don't know where I dropped them, and now my son and husband can never return to the sea." The tears were streaming down her face. "I've already decided that I will leave the sea too, and live ashore with them. But Lachlan will have no protection without me. I want him to come with us, and we'll live up north as we should, as humans. That means I can't have him trying to protect you." She said firmly. "Please ... I've already lost so much family." She squeezed my hands, until I nodded.

The lump in my throat made it hard to swallow, and the tears in her eyes spoke louder than the words. I cleared my throat. "I'll find him for you." My voice was hollow, empty of emotion.

"Thank you, Sahara. I'm ... I am sorry." I just nodded, opened the doors, and called to the octopus nurse. "She's awake, please get Lachlan and some food."

I sat back inside, until I felt the sand move with Lachlan's footprints. I left as he entered, and he ran right to her side.

I headed down the beach toward the spot where I found her, floating near the shore. Kai wasn't far away and ran up to me.

"Hey, Red. You look grim. What's wrong?" He asked.

"Oh, um, Aerwyna woke up." I said absently.

"That's great! Lachlan will be so happy!" He looked at me. "Why aren't you happy? You obviously like Lachlan a lot." So, it was obvious. I sighed. "Aerwyna said she had her husband and son's skins with her when she escaped, but she dropped them sometime after she was stabbed. I'm trying to think of a way to find them."

Kai fiddled with the ring on his finger, then said. "Come on, let's go search." And he ran into the water.

He jumped and his shorts flashed and turned into his signature teal tail and splashed at me. "Come on, Red! Let's see how fast you can swim now"

We dove down to the bottom of the ocean floor and started combing the area.

"Hey Kai, how does that jewelry work?" I asked, interested.

"Huh. Oh. Well, to be totally honest. It's cursed jewelry." He said, as we swam back and forth.

"Cursed jewelry?"

"Yeah. We get it from the Sea-Witch. Unlike what I said originally, not all merfolk can walk on land. Only those wearing cursed jewelry can." He pointed to a shadow on the seafloor ahead.

"So, what happens if you lose the jewelry?" I asked.

"Well, if you lose it, you are stuck in whatever form you are in. So, if you are on land, you stay human. In the sea, you stay sea bound." He swam faster, towards the piles in the sand.

I touched the ocean floor and felt the sands. They whispered in my ear. *There are a lot of creatures swimming this way. You need to go back to the island.*

"Kai, we need to go," I said. He snapped his head back and looked at me. "What do you mean? I think those are the skins ahead. The sands shifted beneath my hand, and the skins were flowing towards me. I grabbed them both and waved at Kai. "Kai, the sands say there is something big coming this way. We need to go. Now."

He grabbed my hand, pulling me along. We swam quickly, and then surfaced, and I called the sands to take us further inland. I had his hand this time, and I called for Phillip. Kai whistled, and soon we were surrounded by the others.

"There is something coming for us in the water." I told them, hugging the skins to my body.

"There are a lot of sea creatures coming." There were some shouts, and then everyone was moving, preparing for the coming battle. I grabbed the skins, and Kai's hand, and went to knock on Aerwyna's door.

Lachlan opened the door and saw us holding hands. He narrowed his eyes, and asked,

"What's going on?" I shoved the skins into his hand, as Kai told him "We were swimming in the water, and we could feel it - there are tons of creatures headed this way. The shifters are prepping for battle." I felt the shift in his demeanor, as he hardened. I heard a siren shout my name, and turned and ran off, leaving Kai and Lachlan to talk battle.

I headed to the pool and saw the sirens. The dolphins had bins of wet towels prepped and ready, in case we needed to move them to the sea.

"What's going on?" I asked breathlessly.

"We can sense something is happening" Brooke said, "How can we help?"

"There's a ton of creatures coming this way. I'm not sure what to say."

"Let us go back into the sea. We are vicious when we need to be." Cordelia said.

"Yes, we can fight back if we need to. But we need access to the sea." Raidne said.

"I don't want to see anyone hurt over this." I said, shaking my head.

"You can't save everyone, darling," Brooke said, grabbing my hands. "Please let us fight for our own lives. We already gave our souls to the sea, let us fight to get them back."

It was the same thing Namiko said. "They will fight for themselves, and their loved ones." I had to let them fight.

"Ok, let's get these sirens to the sea." I leaned into the sand, and made a pathway through the bottom, and out, and then I did the same with the jellyfish, releasing them from the pool into the ocean from the bottom.

"The pool is now deep and has a tunnel out to the sea. You are free to leave or to fight, if you choose." The six of them smiled at me, and thanked me, and dived down into the water..

Ashera looked at me and smiled. "You are very brave, you know." "What?" I asked, confused.

"You are the first person who has ever challenged the queen, and rescued others, and tried to help."

"I was always told that if you can help someone, you should. You never know what they are facing." She smiled at me. "That's true. I'm not sure I ever officially apologized for my actions in keeping the sirens prisoners on the island. I really hope those girls are doing okay." "If these four girls escaped to find me, I'm sure the others are okay."

"Queen Loralei will not let this rest, you know. She will search and attack you until you are defeated." Ashera said. "She will use you as an example. To show what she will do to anyone attempting a revolution. "Then I will become the martyr and spark it further." She smiled, and dove into the pool, following the sirens.

There was a shout out by the beach. The creatures had been spotted surfacing. The battle had begun.

The sand was quivering beneath me, and my legs were equally jellied. I looked out at the water and saw the sheer number of creatures whose heads had popped up. And that didn't account for those who would be beneath the waters.

The winds were blowing into my face, carrying the scents of the ocean with it. I could hear the mumbling, and then heads popped up in front of us. Dolphins, octopi and sirens lined up in front of the land. Those of us still on shore were the few merfolk, the octopi healers, and me.

I sunk into the sand to my calves, bracing for whatever was coming my way. I moved the jellyfish pool slowly with the sands, until they were in a bay formed on the beach. Octavius picked one up and asked, "Is this okay?"

I heard the jellyfish get riled up and shout, "Throw me, baby! Let us attack!" I smiled, and nodded to Octavius, as he handed out the jellyfish very carefully to the octopi in the sea. They were each holding up to four jellyfish, ready to be launched at a moment's notice.

We were armed and ready for this fight. The air filled with tension between both sides, as the sea lapped the shore. The air was still and there would be no advantage from the sea today. She would stay neutral, allowing us to settle our own fates.

I saw Lachlan and Aerwyna hobble out of their hut, their injuries keeping them on land. They had grabbed spears and Aerwyna was holding the knife that had been shoved into her back as a weapon.

A sea turtle surfaced, carrying Queen Loralei with her glorious royal blue tail, still wearing her silver crown studded with sapphires. It appeared almost as if she was the embodiment of the ocean itself. The tides stilled, as we faced each other, both sides ready to die for what they believed.

She called out "Sara, darling, let's you and I have a chat. Having an all-out war over such petty things is frivolous."

"Frivolous? Freeing the sirens from being your slaves is petty and frivolous?" I yelled back.

Kai shook his head. "Don't engage," he whispered. "She'll have brought the sea-witch as backup, I'm sure." I looked at him. That's why the merfolk weren't in the water. The sea-witch would call the jewelry away from them, forcing them to live under her thumb. I looked at the beaches, and saw that each wielded a spear, and many were touching their cursed jewelry. They were willing to stay human to fight for their freedom.

"That's not what I'm talking about. I'm talking about this notion that the ocean is divided. We both really want peace between all creatures." She swept her hand across, showcasing the diversity of her flotilla.

"All the creatures, you say? All those born in the sea are those who live by the rules of the Sea. You've broken those rules. Forced the sirens to do dirty work. Forced the merfolk into finding and creating more sirens. Forced the sharks into being your assassins and forced the rest to make you believe you are in charge. Well, face it. A Queen needs her people. Not the other way around."

"I see we are getting nowhere with you," she turned to her waiting flotilla, and issued her orders. "Kill the sirens. The rest I can beat into submission but kill whoever gets in your way. I will take the red bitch out." Then there was a flurry of motion as an army of shark fins moved towards the beach.

Octavius shouted "LAUNCH" And the jellyfish screamed their war cries as they landed and started to sting whoever was in reach. The Dolphins pulled nets hidden in the sand dunes and trapped sharks in place. The net wouldn't last long as their teeth would eventually rip through it. The merfolk launched arrows at us, and the squids shot ink into the sea, turning it a nasty black colour, obscuring the sights above and below. The greasy substance coated everything, and the creatures were slipping and swerving, careening out of control. The sirens went into action, tearing into the sharks as they escaped the net. The dolphins bit and chomped at the turtles and squid and forced her army back from the shore.

Queen Loralei picked her way through the fighting, arriving ashore on the back of her sea turtle, the royal guards following her. She reached up and touched her crown, as she transformed into a human shape..

"Her cursed jewelry is her crown," I said to Kai. He nodded, understanding, then raised his spear.

"FOR FREEDOM!" He yelled. We all charged towards the invading merfolk; spears raised. I let the sand carry me and it felt like I was flying toward her. I dodged past her guards, as I had in the palace, with the sand as my ally. All around me I heard cries and the clash of spears against spears.

Loralei strutted forward confidently and pulled out a trident that extended with the push of a button. She sneered at my empty hands as she raised it toward me. "You didn't think the queen would come unprepared to fight for herself, did you?"

I lifted the sand and formed it into my own spear, holding it steady and solid in my arms. I felt Kai come up beside me and raise his spear to her.

"Oh, Kai. Araxie and Melody will be so disappointed in you. Your parents will have to be hung out to dry." She said as she swung the trident at him.

He dodged the incoming blow, as more merfolk reached the shore. I pushed the sand up and created a high bank, putting us on a sheer cliffside. I looked out to the beach below. Namiko was battling another mermaid, spears clashing, Aerwyna and Lachlan were fighting off several guards, on land, back-to-back. Octavius had three sharks head-locked in his tentacles and Phillip was leading the dolphins in squid-tossing. Loralei launched Kai back, and he fell down the cliffside. He was surrounded by guards but fell back into step with Namiko.

"Well, Miss Red-Siren. It's just you and me now.

I dug my feet in and enclosed us in a ring of sand.

She swung hard, and clipped my sand spear with her trident, and it collapsed as I lost concentration. She swung again, and I dodged.

"Keep dodging. But I will get you." She thrust forward, again and again. I kept dodging and knocked her trident back with my own sand spear. She nicked me a couple times, the blood dripping from my arms. Her eyes were lost in a frenzy, similar to what I had seen in the sirens, the day we downed the boat. She wasn't in control. A monster was. She was thrusting more wildly, losing control of her own power.

I sank down to my waist in the sands and thrust my sand spear towards her legs. She tripped over it and fell forward but used her trident to catch her fall. With her trident in the sand, I solidified it, holding it steady. Then I shouted down the cliffside,

"START SINGING!"

Loralei struggled to pull her trident out of the sand, and I raised myself up. I loosened the sand beneath her, watching her wriggle and try to get out. I swung my spear at her, knocking the crown from her head and watched it fall into the sea.

Her eyes widened as it tumbled down, and she realised she was trapped. She fought with the sand, and the siren song grew strong and loud. The merfolk were launching themselves from the cliffs into the water below. As the last of them jumped, the dolphins and octopi were netting and roping them in.

"Bring those with jewelry ashore. Once they have transformed, take their jewelry." I called.

Kai looked at me as blood seeped from his leg. There were a couple of cuts across his chest.

Lachlan and Aerwyna were embracing and holding each other up but looked unharmed.

The octopi healers were bringing in the injured and working to save lives.

"Where's the sea-witch?" I asked a still-trapped Loralei. She laughed, a high shrill manic laughter.

"You think you've won? Oh no. There's no winning. I didn't bring her. But she will come for you. She will come for you." She laughed and laughed.

"If you think I'm the biggest tyrant in the ocean you are dead wrong." Her eyes flashed, and her expression wavered between mania and confusion. I lowered the sands and recreated the beach. The sharks had slowed their frenzied snapping and the sirens had stopped singing. The sea was red and black and moaning.

"Your queen is trapped. And her crown has been buried in the sea floor. Her reign of the merfolk ends now." I called out to the mass of creatures. There was cheering and rejoicing, and I even noticed some of those that arrived with the queen were embracing those that were on the island.

I slumped in the sand, and sat there, marvelling at the magnitude of what I had done and what we had accomplished as a united group. We could hear Loralei's maniacal laughter in the sand, even as Phillip and Octavius came to tie her and carry her away.

After they retrieved her, and all the cursed jewelry, I checked on the sirens. All seven of them had made it back, though they weren't without injury. A few sirens had shark teeth embedded in various body parts, and some had gashes that needed to be treated. Maya looked up at me with concern in her eyes.

"Are you okay, Sahara?" She asked. I sat down and dipped my feet into the pool and looked at the soulless women who had more heart and fight in them than any friends I've ever met.

"I just don't understand why I'm so different from you. I mean, I can transform."

"That's because you're half human." Raidne said.

"I can speak underwater?"

"I'm pretty sure that's because you didn't give your voice in service to the sea." Pasha answered.

"I can understand the sea creatures and talk to them?" I shot back.

"Oh. We can all understand the fish and jellies. Those guys are funny as hell. Swearing and cursing the mer-folk for using them. I'm not surprised they chose to fight her." Cordelia said.

"Wait ... you can all understand the animals?"

"Of course. We can hear the shifters in human form, but not in animal. We can't talk to them at all because we are muted underwater. And talking to fish above water is mostly them screaming for help." Nixie said.

"You are definitely a siren." Brooke said, "you are half human though, and took on traits from your father. The tenacity, and the will to survive. That's your father." She smiled wistfully.

"Okay, so if most of these weird things *can* be explained by being a hybrid or whatever. How do you explain the sands?"

"The desert siren" a male voice said behind me. I turned and stared at Kai, as he limped in. "That's what your girlfriends called you on land, the Desert Siren, right?" He asked.

"Yes, because I grew up in the desert, away from all water, and never seeing the ocean."

"Water is everywhere, Sahara. Even in the desert. The sea has always called to you, even in her smallest form. " He smiled and sat down beside me.

"You are capable of moving the sands because you are born of land and of sea. You have a strong pull to the sea, and the seas are everywhere. Since you were never near water, she had to get creative to link herself to you ... at least, that would be my biggest theory." He smiled and looked around the room.

"Is everyone okay?" They all nodded, as he stood. "I'm making the rounds, checking in on all the people. Also, is it true you can hear all the animals speak? Even the fish?"

"Yeah. They have some interesting lives too." Maya said, her voice squeaking. Kai raised his hands to his ears. "Sorry!" She switched to a throatier sound and lower register. Kai put his thumb up.

"That's really interesting. You will have to tell me the stories they tell. And also, what we are doing to them that they don't like. It's not fair to be forced to do things you don't want." Then he turned and left, continuing to help the others.

"Is it just me, or would he make a great leader?" Nixie asked. Always straight to the point with that one.

"He would. And he's so cute, too!" Pasha chimed in.

"Eh, I don't care for Mermen. Or men in general for that matter," signed Constance. The cut to her throat had damaged her vocal chords, and she would likely never use her voice again.

"And yet you fought so hard to stay out of the colosseum." Cordelia teased back. "A whole room of them, and you wouldn't come stay with us."

"I was trying to keep the girls on Donut Island safe. I really hope they're all okay," she signed back.

"Oh, that's right. Loralei said she wasn't the end of this, and that the sea witch would stop us. Do you know anything?"

"Octavius, Phillip and Lachlan will have some of those answers, Sweetie. You should check with the ambassadors," Brooke told me.

"Thanks, I will." I took off as the girls continued to talk about how cute Kai was. And they had a point. Kai was cute, smart and sweet and...

My thoughts dropped off as I heard arguing.

"You told her what? How could you make that choice for me? That wasn't your decision!"

"You don't see it! She's dangerous to you. To us. To the selkies. She will get everyone around us killed." Aerwyna. I stopped in my tracks.

"Andrew and Archie's skins are still missing. They are still out gods-knows-where on land, still enslaved by that stupid queen's rule. I need your help to find them. To find the skins. She doesn't need you. I do."

I could hear the desperation in her voice as it wavered.

"You need me, like you've always needed me. And I'll always help you, dear sister. But still, you can't push her away from me. If I have to push her away to help you stay safe, I will. I will always protect you, like I always have, when Dad died protecting us. But it's still my choice, please."

My heart broke as he argued. And right then I knew that he would

choose her over me. It was his right. She was his sister, and I was nothing but an oddity, an interest, and someone he had known for all of a week. I left them to their argument and went to find Octavius. Instead, I found Phillip, hanging out nude near a tree.

"Nothing is fair in love and war, and darling, I'm afraid you can't win both." I looked up at him, since looking down meant a face full of dolphin dick I wasn't really interested in viewing.

"Thanks for that lovely insight, Phillip. I'm looking for Octavius. I think there might be more battles to fight in this war. Have you seen him? Or a pair of shorts? "

"What, you don't like my nudity? Bet you can't get enough of the seals though. Damn Selkies." He laughed but turned and pointed to the southern section.

"I saw Octavius headed in that direction with the land bound queen, Kai and Namiko. They wanted to interrogate her royal madness. And if it pleases you, I will find some pretty cloth to wrap around these excellent loins. "

"Make sure to tie the cloth in a tight bow, it'll be a gift for some woman someday, I'm sure." I called as I wandered down the isle

"It could be yours!"

"You wish." Damned horny dolphins.

I reached Octavius, Kai and Namiko in no time, but they were pointing at something in the distance that I couldn't see.

"Where is Loralei?" I asked them, confused since she should have been with them, according to Phillip.

"She's in a room, laughing her head off, but we were flagged by some octopi about a ship sailing into our territory. It's unusual to see ships out here, so she's either totally lost, or she's intentionally sailing this way." Octavius said.

"Do you need Loralei?" Kai asked.

"Well, both you and she mentioned the Sea-Witch." I mused out loud. "My mother - that sounds weird to me - Brooke, said that Octavius might have some information, as well as Loralei."

"A sea-witch? There are only a handful of them, and they keep to themselves usually." Octavius thought. "But which witch?"

"What do you mean which witch?" Namiko asked. "There is only one sea-witch that I know of."

"Yeah, Samruda." Kai said.

"Shhh, do not speak their name. They can scry and spy on us from afar if their names are spoken," Octavius shushed Kai. "Let's go speak with our landlocked queen of the sea and see if we can find out anything more." We followed him to the screened-in room and heard her laughing from far back. It was loud and maniacal.

"She's coming for you." She said as we entered the room.

"Who is coming for me?" I asked her pointedly.

"The witch, the witch, she comes. She doesn't need me anymore." She burst into giggles.

"Is - is she okay?" I asked Octavius.

"It seems her brain has been tampered with, and whatever or whoever she was is locked underneath this facade. Sea-Witches are powerful spellcasters."

"Loralei, are you in there?" Namiko asked quietly. "It's me, Loralei, Namiko. You, me, and Melody used to play together. We grew up together." She continued to try and reach her, as we looked on.

"The crown controls, the one who wears the crown controls the sea. The sea is controlled by the crown, the witch has the crown. The witch is the crown. The crown, the crown, it's all to do with the crown." Then she shook and began to scream incoherent babble. We backed out of the room and stood in contemplation.

I could feel his footprints in the sand, as he was coming toward us, and I didn't want to face him.

"I think I should get her crown from the sea floor" I said, and then raced off towards the eastern edge of the island, passing Lachlan as he walked up to the others.

"Sahara, wait..." He called, but I kept going, leaving them all there, dumbfounded as the sand carried me to the beach. I waded into the water, and then dove down to the sea floor, ignoring the world above. I let the water fill my lungs and surround me as I fell into the cool sea.

I would have to leave this world, and that's okay. I would return to my desert, and finish my doctorate, and mentor the school choir. Their voices would never compare to the siren's voices, but I could go back. I needed to tell my dad I was still alive. Oh my god, my dad. I could reunite him with Mom, and ... and then what? She was sea-bound still unless we could find a Sea-Witch to bestow her cursed jewelry. The crown!

I could give her cursed jewelry. I could give her the crown.

I put my hands on the ocean floor and used my senses to feel for the crown I buried. The sand whispered to me: *This crown isn't for your mother. Do not put it on another's head, Sahara. Seek out the secluded witch and bring her the crown, she will help to stop the tyranny, and help Loralei remember who she is.*

"But why can't I give this to my mother, and bring her home to my father? She'll be safe there. "

Your father is close, the other sirens have listened to me and brought his ship here. I am not an unfair mistress, Sahara. I want my sirens to help the sailors on the sea. I am not the one seeking the souls. You must find and stop the true tyrant in the sea.

"I thought I did." and then I sat on the bottom of the ocean, fiddling with the silver and sapphire crown. Do I bring it up, or do I leave it buried? I felt the sea floor, looking for a satchel or bag in the sands, and felt something come forward. I inspected the red satchel and stuck the crown inside.

"Thank you, Mistress" I told the sea.

Be safe, Sahara, it will take all of you to win this war.

And then I was being pushed out of the sea and up onto the beach. I coughed as I transformed quicker than I anticipated, but the red satchel carrying the crown stayed across my waist. I tightened it, and turned back to the southern side, ready to tell them all to stand down.

Suddenly my arm was being grabbed, and I was spun right into Lachlan's chest. He wrapped his arms around me and hugged me tight. I lifted my hands to his chest and pushed.

"Sahara, what's wrong?" He asked, letting me go.

"You know exactly what's wrong. You're leaving me." His face flashed with emotions, and then he hardened, as I continued. "You're going to go get your nephew and brother-in-law. I know. I heard you and Aerwyna this afternoon. You should go find your family. The skins I gave you, those are theirs. Kai and I picked them up off the sea floor just before the battle. Now just go, so I don't have to pretend that I don't want you to choose me."

I didn't look at him, and I tried to spin away from him.

His finger was under my chin, and he lifted my face up to look into his eyes. There were tears in them as he leaned down to put his forehead against mine. "Sahara, I will always choose you," He whispered into my ear, "if I have the power to choose." He tied my hair back using the hair tie around his wrist. "I know you retrieved their skins, and there is absolutely no way to thank you for the gift you have given my family."

I leaned into him, tears falling from my face, as he gently placed his lips against mine, and kissed me like it was our last kiss. The sea sent a breeze and the sand quivered beneath us. The taste of salt was bitter this time as he pulled away and wiped the tears from my eyes.

"Go find your family. Bring them back to the ocean safely." I choked out. "And keep Aerwyna safe." I dropped my hand and forced myself away from him. He took a step away, headed back to the shelter where he and his sister had stayed. "I will find you again, Lass." He would be okay, they would find their family, and be reunited. I had another family to reunite, my own.

I burst into the siren's pool room, breathing heavily. "Ship. Southern. Coast. Dad." I spit out, and the girls looked at me confused. I lifted my hands and signed, "DAD. SHIP. SOUTH." Brooke's eyes widened, and she immediately dove deep into the pool, and out the tunnel. The sirens gave me a look. I took a few more breaths before I could sort my thoughts into plain language."T he other sirens followed the call of the sea and brought my dad's ship here." I told them.

Nixie's eyes widened. "My sisters!" and then there was a great deal of splashing and diving that suddenly emptied the pool.

Running to the southern beach, I called to Octavius, "That's my father's ship, and it's being led by the rest of the sirens who followed directions from the Sea."

Octavius called out a few commands, and then I saw the siren's heads pop out of the water, as they jumped and swam towards the ship. Leading the way, I could see Brooke's orange-brown tail.

"Octavius, I have another question to ask you. What do you know about the secluded sea-witch?"

He looked at me in surprise and nodded. "I suppose there is something special about you. She is another sea-witch that hasn't been seen in a very long time. A sea-serpent who lives in seclusion from other sea creatures, choosing to use her magic to heal those who need it. Her last known location was in squid territory, at the base of a sea stack. I believe the squids call it Dolomite Stack. It is a far distance, and dangerous to get there. Especially if the squids are still loyal to Queen Loralei."

"She'll be coming with me." I stated. Shock filled his face as he tried to grasp what I said.

"Her brain is broken, and it has something to do with the sea-witch, and this crown" I tapped my satchel. "The sea told me to take Loralei to the secluded sea-witch to remember who she is. So, I am going to take her. On that ship." I pointed to my father's approaching ship, and the dozens of sirens floating around it.

I felt Kai's footsteps in the sand and whipped around. "You aren't stopping me, either." I pointed my finger at him. He held his hands up and smiled.

"I'm not fighting with you, Troublemaker; I want to come with you. Namiko, and a few of the others are going to return to the island to try and break their families out of Araxia's Manor. You gave them the confidence to fight back, Red. I have no idea where they are holding my parents, but I can help with Loralei, and get her memory back. Let's go sailing, Troublemaker." He smiled cheekily, and then dove into the water to help pull the moderately sized boat, a small yacht, with room for a handful of people.

My father jumped down into the ocean and ran to me on the shore. We were in a deep embrace, when I saw Brooke in the sea, smiling and crying. I turned him around and led him to her. When he saw her, he crumpled to his knees in the shallow water, tears streaming down his face. She went to him and pulled him into a deep embrace, and then kissed my dad. I could feel the tears on my own cheeks. I've never seen my dad this happy. He signed to her *"I love you. All this time, you've been okay?"*

Brooke nodded. "I missed you. I love you." I let them hug and catch up for a bit, as the sirens shared the stories about what happened to each side as I set them free. My dad got up and pulled me towards Brooke. I smiled at her and held their hands. "I'm happy for you both." I signed, "but Dad, we need your ship to find a sea-witch. She could grant Mom her legs and help to heal the broken queen."

"I will sail with my daughter and my wife." "Dad, we will swim. I need you to take the queen who can't turn back into a mermaid.*"

He nodded and looked at Brooke. *"You are coming with me again. And I won't let you out of my sight this time."*

Cordelia called to the sirens. "The sea has given you your missions, listen only to the sea, and your hearts. If you need help, call the creatures of the sea to pass along the message and we will be there to help one another."

Octavius and Phillip helped us bring the still muttering Loralei onto my father's ship. At least my father is deaf and can't hear the craziness.

I climbed up with my father and introduced him to Kai. Kai and he signed quite a bit, and soon my dad was showing him how to sail the ship. I searched the waters for Lachlan and Aerweyna, knowing that he would have taken off as soon as he could after that sad kiss.

We would be together again someday, I thought.

Octavius and Phillip donned their skins, and followed us into the water, swimming with us as the ship started sailing. I looked down as my mother swam beside the ship. I dove down into the water, passing through a sand dune and began swimming beside her. We would all be on land together soon. The journey was just beginning.

J essie Sadler is the Blizzard Queen. Hailing out of
Winnipeg, she has been known to freeze her butt
off during the frigid winters. She spends that icy season
filling notebooks with ideas, stories, and characters who
have a tale to tell. With some reluctance, she stepped out
onto the thin ice of sharing her work publically. The ice
cracked, and she was plunged into a new world.

She brought her first characters to life, writing in a literary magazine, InThePantheon.com as Khione, the Goddess of Snow. Jessie takes pride in bringing her characters off the page and making readers feel emotionally connected. Since the first plunge, she has had some poems published, and a blog filled with her short stories and musings.

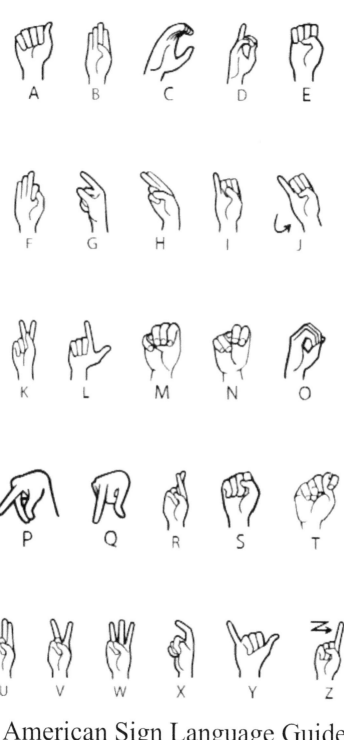

American Sign Language Guide

Printed in the USA
CPSIA information can be obtained
at www.ICGtesting.com
JSHW062148151023
49994JS00009B/53